THE ʼ

CW01085427

"Twopence stood as if to catch him should he fall again"
(see page 28).

THE
TWINS AT SCHOOL

Evelyn Smith

Books to Treasure

Books to Treasure
5 Woodview Terrace,
Nailsea, Bristol, BS48 1AT
UK

www.bookstotreasure.co.uk
www.facebook.com/BooksToTreasure

First published by Cassel & Company 1927
This edition 2018

Design and layout © Books to Treasure

ISBN 978-1-909423-92-3

CONTENTS

PREFACE

Constance Evelyn Smith was born in Leamington Spa on 27 December 1885, the eldest of three daughters to Henry Barlett Smith and his wife Eleanor. She attended Leamington High School, where she rose to become head of school, and gained her first-class degree in English from Royal Holloway College. In 1909 Evelyn went to teach English at Glasgow High School but ill health forced her resignation in 1923. She died on 23 March 1928.

The Twins at School

CHAPTER I

THE TWINS' FIRST DAY AT SCHOOL

A nd your name?"

Miss Blencowe, of Form Lower Third, paused, having delivered her question with the right degree of briskness to inspire energy, sharpness to enforce discipline, and pleasantness to hearten a probably diffident new pupil. The form, anxious to hear what might proceed from the lips of the girl in the front row, was unusually silent. It could see only her back, but it approved of the bracken-gold hair, rippling in a line that no permanent wave can achieve, as a few people in their 'teens, who had begun to think of such things, knew.

"Penny," came the answer in a voice that was charming while, as the occasion demanded, shy.

"Excuse me, your full name."

"Oh, I'm sorry. Penelope. Penelope Lilian Wood."

"Quite. And yours?" The mistress, recording swiftly as the dryad-like figure sank into the ugly, shiny seat again, turned to the next desk, whose occupant scrambled eagerly to her feet and leaned forward with a confidential expression that, directed towards this particular Miss Blencowe, would have amused the rest of the class if they could have seen it.

"Twopence."

A giggle from the back row was instantly suppressed by a look in Miss Blencowe's eye.

"Excuse me!"

The small girl with the bobbed hair cut like that of a medieval page turned with the intention of completing the good work begun on the back row, but, finding all was well, again put herself at the disposal of the mistress.

"Twopence!" she boomed in the deep voice that came surprisingly from so inconsiderable a chest. "Twopence Wood."

Miss Blencowe looked hurt.

"Impossible!" she declared.

There was a short silence. The new-comer, who had claimed the unheard right to be known as Twopence Wood, thrust her chin forward and regarded this power confronting her. She disliked powers, especially new ones. She disliked what she called an indoor face, and she very much disliked a black velvet bow, ornamented with pen-painted flowers and fastened with a fancy brooch at the neck of a shirt blouse. Civilized society, while recognizing the possible existence of such aversions, does not permit them to be openly shown, but Twopence Wood frequently refused to recognize this fact. Her twin sister, looking at her doubtfully, slowly raised an explanatory hand.

"It's her pet name," she volunteered, as Miss Blencowe seemed to grant permission. "I'm Penny, you see, short for Penelope, and she's Twopence. The point is that we're twins."

Miss Blencowe, by mere gesture, conveyed to the form that, in regarding this piece of information as a joke, they were mistaken.

The stubborn twin faced round upon the beautiful one.

"Don't interfere, Penny!" she said. "It's *my* name, and it isn't anything to do with you or yours. And I *am* called Twopence," she again informed the mistress, "and I have been for eleven years, so it *must* be possible."

A flush of anger crept up under Miss Blencowe's skin, turning it a dull rhubarb colour.

"What is *not* possible for a girl in this school, my dear," she enunciated, "is impertinence."

Twopence blazed. She hated the charge of "impertinence" as much as she hated being called "my dear." If she had been taxed with insolence and addressed as a limb of Satan she would have agreed to the justice of the accusation and subsided into docility.

"Isn't it?" she questioned.

Penelope's grey eyes besought Miss Blencowe to forgive, to forget, to leave her sister alone. The Lower Third stared doubtfully at the defiant back and the small clenched hands. Blenks, as they called her, was a nuisance, but they were not sure whether a new girl had a right to think so. Besides, this new girl was not suffering from high spirits, the sin for which they were used to being punished, but from temper, which they did not understand so well. They inclined towards dislike for Twopence Wood.

Miss Blencowe cleared her throat and adjusted the pen-painted tie.

"Penelope, take your place," she commanded, pointing to a vacant desk in the back row. "And you"—to Twopence—"go out of the room."

Penelope gasped, turning towards her sister. For a minute the two looked at one another, then Penelope went quietly to the seat indicated, and Twopence approached the door. She flung it open with violence, and closed it as gently as if the Lower Third had been very ill invalids. Miss Blencowe sighed with relief. For the first time in her confident life she had not expected to be obeyed.

Outside in the long green corridor Twopence leaned against the wall, physically shaken with rage—the dreadful rage that was always coming upon her from nowhere, and that never, never touched Penny. Beneath the pain of the red-hot hammers that seemed to beat in her head she was conscious of a miserable fact that would hurt more when the hammers had stopped—the fact that Penny was inside and she was out.

It had always been like that—Penelope allowed to stay up for dinner, Twopence sent early to bed; Penelope sitting at the table in the sunny schoolroom window at home, listening to the wisdom of a governess, Twopence glaring in sullen wretchedness from the corner of shame; Penelope swung on to the saddle behind one of her stepfather's friends, Twopence trudging the dull, straight mile before the gates of their house; Penelope easy and happy with boys and girls at a rare party, Twopence somehow estranged and out of it. There must have been some reason— Twopence could never remember how the unhappy thing began. It just seemed to happen, as it had happened to-day.

That hateful woman! Those hateful girls! Twopence thought angrily of the expectant eyes and friendly looks of the occupants of the back row as they made room for her sister. School was evidently to be a miserable experience—and she and Penelope had meant it to be a happy one.

Up to now they had had some happy times, though theirs had been a queer life. They could not remember their father. For three years after his death their mother had lived in a crumbling yellow villa set in the olive and cypress trees beyond Fiesole, and her baby girls played with little Florentines and spoke an odd mixture of baby Italian and English. Then she married Ian Muirhead, an artist friend of her brother, who came to Florence to paint and made the hospitable yellow villa his headquarters. The six-year-old twins liked the bleak old house, backed with mountains and faced by the shining, dangerous waters of one of the most beautiful of the West of Scotland lochs, which was their next home, but their delicate mother, acclimatized to the warm country where she had spent most of her life, contracted pneumonia during the hard Northern winter, and died ten months after her second marriage. The education of the children was provided by a succession of instructors—now a French mademoiselle, now a decorous lady of the old school who had taught the daughters of an Italian prince, now a young graduate from Girton, now the village pedagogue, who came up to Tigh-na-Mara for a couple of hours when his daily labours were ended. Their stepfather occasionally gave them a drawing lesson, laughing at them both, but rather pleased with Twopence, as she always knew with surprise and delight. Between these educational episodes—no one taught the twins for long, to Ian's vague annoyance—were days, weeks, months of splendid freedom. He told them all sorts of stories when he was in the mood; they painted strange figures and scenes on his old canvases; they climbed, fished, swam and sailed, made a few enemies and many friends in the clachan, and entered their twelfth year with a varied and, from a high school's point of view, a useless set of accomplishments. They knew a little Italian and Gaelic, but no Latin or French; they had heard the fairy tales of Europe, but could not have analysed an English sentence nor parsed an English verb; they could play a salmon and reef a sail, but were ignorant of the rules of hockey and lacrosse. They learned what they liked, and Ian, who did the same, was satisfied. Then he married again, and the new Mrs. Muirhead said that the twins were darlings, but had run wild, and that it was his duty to send them to a thoroughly good English boarding-school. There was Queen Æthelfleda's, for instance, on the edge of Warwickshire, her old school. It would do, wouldn't it? He thought it would, and so the twins were hurried to Glasgow, provided with school outfits, and sent off via the Caledonian and London and North-Western to the middle of England.

They did not feel they had been treated cruelly by Maynie, as they called their stepmother, who had been a Miss Maynard. She was rather flatteringly amused by them and did not interfere with their pursuits; she couldn't help being afraid of the loch; and they liked her fair hair and her clothes, especially the things she wore in the evening. They had never known their stepfather well; it was on one another, on stories, and on the big world of moor, mountain and water that they had depended. Wherever they went there would be those exciting outside things, they supposed, and they were to go to school together. They were interested in having a stepfather and a stepmother—even in tales they had not heard of heroines in such a predicament. They liked themselves, they liked life, and they meant to like school.

So far Penelope had not been disappointed. On the first night the twins had slept by themselves in a room with yellow curtains called the Primrose Dormitory, and the gay, clean simplicity of its furnishings had appealed to her, though Twopence could vouchsafe no further comment than a taciturn "It isn't ugly." The few girls they had seen before bedtime had hardly spoken to them, but Penelope thought they looked kind, and indeed her shy, attractive smile had made it impossible for them to appear otherwise. Twopence, piqued because they were discussing things that neither she nor her twin could understand, had scowled at them, and they had regarded her coldly and critically. She had decided that she did not like girls. Her first experience in the classroom inclined her to think that she did not like mistresses any better.

The remembrance of Miss Blencowe's scathing "Impossible!" came back and stung her again. What right had the person in the pen-painted tie to say that? What right had she to sentence her to stand in this dull, cold corridor, with its row of shut doors?

What was that? A storm of guttural and spluttering sounds from the door behind her made Twopence fairly jump, and as thirty voices, attempting in docile unison to get the exact pronunciation of a German irregular verb, continued to smite her ears, her astonishment gave way to further indignation.

"Silly *asses!*" she thought. "How *can* they go on like that? I simply shan't stand it."

And, putting her resolution into action, she walked softly and determinedly down the long corridor, descended a flight of white stone stairs, crossed a quadrangle, and entered the dormitory block.

In two minutes she was in the room where she and Penelope had slept the night before. From the cupboard facing her bed she extracted a short, fat diary she used as a sketch-book, and a box of bull's-eyes. There was a shilling in her pocket. Thus equipped, she was ready to face the world—at any rate, until her present fit of rage was over. Like many older and more experienced people, she couldn't think beyond that.

As she turned to the door her eyes fell on the small wooden shields fixed to the panels. On the lowest were four freshly painted names:

FALCONER, GEORGINA.

MANNERING, LYNETTE M.

WOOD, PENELOPE L.

WOOD, THEODORA.

She and Penelope had been rather pleased with that particular shield last night, and had speculated with interest on the shadowy personalities of Falconer, Georgina, and Mannering, Lynette M., but the sight of it now increased her anger. She wasn't Wood, Theodora, she was Twopence Wood, whatever Queen Æthelfleda or Miss Blencowe might say to the contrary. The sooner that was made plain the better.

The obstinate thrust of the chin came again as Twopence took a penknife from her pocket, and, opening the door, peered out. The corridor was clear. As noiselessly as she could she carefully scratched out the obnoxious Theodora.

"That settles it!" she thought with satisfaction, replacing the knife and surveying the long straight scar which showed where her Christian name had been. "Now for the right one."

There was lamp-black in her water-colour box—no, that wouldn't do. If she could scratch out paint, so could the authorities of Queen Æthelfleda's. It should be a little more difficult than that.

The school building was an old one, unequipped with radiators and electric light; consequently there was an open grate, with fire-irons, in the Primrose Dorm. Twopence lighted her candle, heated the poker red-hot, and, with speed born of natural dexterity, printed her pet name on the blank she had made.

"That'll show her if it's possible," she thought in triumph.

And pulling on the brightly coloured "onion-boy" cap which was Queen Æthelfleda's regulation headgear in winter, she crept down the stairs, out of the front door, which always stood open, along the drive.

"S-s-s-scat!"

Twopence skipped behind a laurel as a door was violently thrown open, and, with a fury born of thoroughly righteous indignation, a black coil was flung into the bushes opposite her hiding-place. The door banged, and with an angry snarl the coil untightened, humped its back, shook itself, and, creeping on to the narrow turf border, looked with wrathful astonishment at the point of its undignified exit.

"Puss!" whispered Twopence, stretching an ingratiating hand. "Puss, puss!"

The puss stared to right and left and just beyond Twopence. Then slowly, as if he did not see her, he approached her laurel bush.

"Poor wee thing!" comforted Twopence, in a voice so gentle that Miss Blencowe would not have recognized it. And her compassionate eyes examined the lean black sides, and the bitten left ear, which looked like a piece of shrivelled leather, as her kind little hand found the exact place under the chin where an insulted cat likes to be tickled. "You shall just come along with me."

And gently lifting him in her arms, she went noiselessly down the turf border, through the big iron gates into the strange lane leading to unknown places.

They wanted her to be outside? Very well, outside she would be.

CHAPTER II

Twopence out of Bounds

"I SAY, I'm dreadfully sorry about your sister."

Penelope turned from the window of the Primrose Dormitory. It was past midday dinner—a meal uncomfortably agitated by anxiety of authorities as to the whereabouts of Twopence. Some mistresses were now searching school bounds, others had hurried down to the little town to question and warn policemen and stationmaster. The twin sister alone seemed undisturbed. She smiled as her room-mate, whose lively features were composed to something like concern, spoke her little piece of sympathy.

"It's really all right," she said. "She'll come back when she doesn't feel angry. Miss Blencowe made her furious, you know. I saw it coming on, and I simply willed and willed something to stop it. But my will wasn't strong enough, I suppose. It's a pity—the first day."

"I know. And if once Blenks takes a dislike to you—. Your name is Penelope, isn't it? I'm Archie Falconer. Georgina, really, but Archie for short. I 'spect you've seen my name on the door." And she turned to look at the shield.

Penelope looked too.

"Och!" she gasped.

"I say!" ejaculated Archie.

"Och, why did Twopence think of doing that?" cried Penelope, now really troubled. "That *shows*. She won't be able to cover it up when she's better. What *is* to be done?"

She looked hopelessly at Archie, who, thoughtfully trying to suppress the joy she couldn't help feeling at the receipt of a good piece of excitement so early in the term, shook her head gravely.

"We'll consult Lynette," she said. "I can hear her in the distance."

Penelope, listening, was conscious of five or six sneezes following one another with distressing rapidity. Then the door opened and another girl came in. She was rather plump, her smooth head was the colour of moor grass, her face was hidden in a large blue silk handkerchief, but when it emerged it showed eyes like brown water and a dimple.

"Hallo!" she said. "I'b Lydedde Badderig. I'b sorry aboud this cold in by head, bud I always ged theb id the traid. An affligshud, bud nod idfeggious, udfortudately for adywud who wads a few days off. Bud please dod tigg I talk like this always."

"She does," said Archie in a loud confidential whisper. "But pretend you don't notice it. She's dreadfully sensitive about it. A new mistress wrote her name in the register as Badderig."

"I dow," said Lynette. "Id's a shabe thad by nabe has so bady ebs ad eds id it. Lydedde Badderig is rather a dice dabe really, ad stradgers always thig id souds ugly." And Lynette tried to look depressed, which, curiously, her cold hadn't made her do.

"I think it's a lovely name," said Penelope politely.

"Do you really? I'b so glad. And your dabe is Bedelobe? I bide have guessed a new girl would be called Bedelobe. Id's just by luck."

"Look what her sister has done to the door!" cried Archie exultingly.

Lynette tried to whistle, but sneezed instead.

"You heard the row with Blenks?" Archie hurried to say. "This is the sequel."

"Is it sure to be found out?" asked Penelope. Her voice was so sad that the others looked at her in consternation.

"I'b afraid id is," said Lynette, before Archie had time to state her opinion. "Bud your sister has rud away, has'd she? I subbose she was frighded after she had dode id."

"Oh, no," said Penelope. "I'm sure she wasn't. Twopence isn't afraid because of anything she does. She has run away because she hates everyone and wants to be alone. No one need waste time looking for her. When she feels better she'll come back."

"Dubbeds!" groaned Lynette. "Id's a codsbiracy."

"Her real name is Theodora," explained Penelope. "We've given up my pet name almost, but not hers. 'Dora' would be quite easy for you to say, but she would hate it so. 'Theodora' she wouldn't have minded, I'm sure, if only she hadn't got angry with Miss Blencowe."

"Bleggs will busd whed she sees thad door," prophesied Lynette as cheerfully as physical limitations would allow.

"Och!" cried Penelope, clasping her hands. "Can't anything be done? Poor Twopence! They'll all be angry with her when she comes back as it is, without this."

"Sobethigg busd be dode," agreed Lynette. "Bleggs busd'd busd. Id sibbly wod do."

"Shut up!" said Archie. "It's really a serious business."

Penelope gave her a grateful look. Then her face suddenly lightened.

"I know!" she said. "If only we could get that shield off the door—a screw-driver would do it—we could varnish the other side and paint the names on as they were done before."

"Gread schebe!" said Lynette.

"Won't the space be noticed?" asked Archie doubtfully. In common with the rest of the Lower Third, she had been repelled by the furious Twopence, but she liked Penelope, and did not want her to get into trouble.

"It's a risk, of course. But, don't you see, it's only a risk of a few days, and to leave the shield as it is would be a risk for ever."

"Thad's sedse," Lynette remarked approvingly. And producing

a pearl-handled penknife, she attempted to raise the shield from its place on the panel.

"Oh, we must get a proper tool," said Archie. "You'll break that silly little blade, Lyn, and the bit will be discovered sticking in the shield. That's the sort of thing that brings men to the gallows."

Lynette looked hurt, but pocketed the knife.

"Couldn't we borrow a screw-driver?" suggested Penelope.

Archie wrinkled her forehead. She prided herself on usefulness in an emergency, and felt it incumbent on her to make a sensible suggestion.

"There are the prefects," she said cautiously. "It's quite likely that there is a packing-case of some sort in their room, as this is the second day of term, and a packing-case means a screw-driver."

"Braid wave!" exclaimed Lynette. "Ad who'll ask theb to led id to us?"

"I will!" cried Penelope. "Where is their room?"

Lynette and Archie looked at one another. The prefects' study was not actually banned to the juniors, but its inhabitants had a way of making anyone who knocked at the door without special invitation feel as if their proper place were on a microscope slide. However, if Penelope Wood didn't mind—

"At the end of the passage," directed Archie. "Straight in front of you, just past that window with the nasturtiums."

Penelope flew off, and without waiting to reflect, turned the handle and walked in.

A lively sound of talk and laughter died down as she stood looking around her. A tall girl with lazy, calm eyes lounged in a big chair by the fireplace, two more occupied a window-seat, and a fourth, with the blackest brows Penelope had ever seen, was kneeling by a wooden packing-case, from which she had just removed the lid.

"Hallo!" said this individual. "Are you the new Sixth Form girl?"

The others stared at her in critical amazement.

Penelope at once knew when she had done the wrong thing, and, rarer gift, she generally saw the right way to undo it. She hesitated now, with a pretty embarrassment. She was not in the least afraid of these big girls, but she instinctively felt they would like her to be—not much, not enough to make her silly or ugly, but enough to make them aware of their own power.

"I am sorry," she said, in her low soft voice, with the West Highland inflection that the last six years had taught her. "I have made a mistake."

"So it is your mistake, is it?" said the black-browed girl, sitting back on her heels and looking quizzically at her.

"Och, yes," said Penelope. "I am only in the Lower Third, but I am wishing a screw-driver."

"I have only a cottage in the country, but I should like the pen of Charles," observed the lazy girl in the arm-chair.

"No," said Penelope, with a serious glance of her charming grey eyes. "I should like the screw-driver of the Sixth."

"Oh. And what special qualification has the Lower Third to deserve the screw-driver of the Sixth?" demanded the black-browed girl.

"None," said Penelope. "But I will gladly give you the loan of anything you wish, at any time."

"That is very good of you."

"Lend the kid the screw-driver, Kate," said the lazy voice from the arm-chair, suddenly authoritative.

"Right, Cynthia."

The black-browed girl rummaged in the shavings, and produced the required tool.

"The point is," she said, handing it to Penelope, who received it like a nymph taking largess from a goddess, "the point is that a Lower Third Former is rather an insignificant type of humanity—even more so than the unimportant beings that call themselves the Sixth."

Penelope looked wistfully round the room.

"I know," she said. "It's these sums that muddle one."

"Sums? Why sums?"

The lazy Cynthia narrowed her grey-green eyes to look at Penelope, who was considering the question snapped out by Kate.

"They teach us," she said, in the gentle, hesitating voice she knew to be effective on an occasion like this, "they teach us that one-third is a bigger fraction than one-sixth."

She did not look, but she knew Cynthia smiled—half a smile, as if she had no energy for more.

"Ah," said Kate, "but we're wholes, not fractions."

"We're fractions of our forms," said Penelope.

"False logic, my child," said Kate. "But take the screw-driver and my blessing; and, when you bring it back, which must be within the next half-hour, put it on the mat, knock at the door, and run away."

"I will remember," said Penelope, and as she softly closed the door she heard an appreciative voice from the window-seat.

"Pretty, isn't she?" it said.

And she smiled her little smile as she went back to the Primrose Dorm—a smile that was not vain nor self-satisfied, only glad because some difficulty had been conquered. Twopence had it too—but it was very rarely that poor Twopence had occasion to use it.

"Oh, yes, they lent it to me," said Penelope, as if surprised that Archie and Lynette seemed so. "There were four of them there," she went on, in answer to Archie's breathed question. "A girl with very black eyebrows—"

"Kate Croydon, the hockey captain!"

"And a nice lazy girl they called Cynthia."

"A nice lazy girl? That's Cynthia Waynfleet—the head girl; and she's tremendously clever, and sometimes she's dreadfully sarcastic."

"I thought she looked nice," said Penelope simply.

"Dice? Dice is'd the word," said Lynette, as enthusiastically as contact with a very damp handkerchief would allow.

"I think Cynthia has a secret sorrow," said Archie, who, Penelope was beginning to notice, had a theory about everyone and everything. "I say—how neatly you've done that!" she added admiringly, as Penelope, deftly handling the screw-driver, removed the shield from the door and wrapped it up in her handkerchief.

"I shall find someone out of school to varnish it," she said. "It must be really well done."

"Every wud dows the Queed Fleda girls," warned Lynette. "You bust be careful."

"Better let me advise you," said Archie.

"Of course I will," said Penelope. "I'll tell you exactly what I have done when I've done it."

Archie thought this over, but was startled into forgetting it by the striking of the little yellow clock on the mantelpiece.

"I say—we're due to play the Postilion d'Amour to Miss Jobberns at three. Come on!"

"Waid a biddude—I busd ged a clead haggerchief. Bother! I have'd god a dry wud."

"I'll lend you one," said Penelope, running to her drawer and producing a big silk one she kept for afflictions such as Lynette's.

"You're wud of the besd," said Lynette gratefully. "I wo'd forged—"

"To borrow it again," finished the heartless Archie. "Come—hustle—"

They dashed off, and Penelope, depressed as soon as she was alone, walked to the window.

Three o'clock! Twopence had been away for five hours—the attack should have worn off by now. Perhaps she had better go out and look for her. These people would not know the likely places. Poor Twopence! Penelope's eyes grew soft as she thought of her—she would have eaten her peppermints, and she would be terribly hungry—she always got terribly hungry. Would they be really cross with her when she came back—or would they be so thankful to see her that they would just be ordinary?

She opened the window of the dorm wider and leaned out. She saw a straight road, leading to a bridge which spanned the lazy, rushy stream flowing past the little town of Queen Æthelfleda, and a straggling path going uphill to a spinney of young oak and beech trees, and a few lean pines, strangely foreign and forsaken-looking in this green gardenish land. ...

"She'll have gone through there," thought Penelope at once. "She'll notice those trees because they look like home."

And she hastily slipped on her coat, because she liked to dig her hands deep into its pockets when she walked, and opened the door.

"I'll find Twopence quite soon," she thought. And, hiding the shield under her coat, she ran quietly out of the school building.

CHAPTER III

IN THE WOODS

"IT is very fortunate, Peter Leathery-Ear, chief of Wee Poor Things, that I found that lost bone for you," said Twopence.

The black cat, seated before a bare and shining bone, yawned and inclined his head a little, as if to express his agreement with this opinion.

"Although I wished you liked peppermints," went on his hostess, shifting hers from one cheek to the other. "There is something wrong about eating peppermints alone."

Peter seemed to think that she should not concern herself on this point, and, with sudden energy, began to wash himself, from the top of his flat head to the leathery pad of each paw.

"I suppose none of the Society of Wee Poor Things will like peppermints," said Twopence thoughtfully. "We do not know yet, Peter, who they will be, but the kind of people anyone like myself will be able to gather together will hardly include peppermint-eaters, I should think."

She gathered up pine-needles in one hand, sniffed them, and looked up through the branches at the sky, which seemed strangely low down, like a big blue curtain stretched over the place where she sat cross-legged, making plans for her new secret society—about which even Penelope would not know.

"They'll all be sad because they find things difficult, or have accidentally done wrong," she went on. "You are a Wee Poor Thing, Peter, because someone has bitten your ear, and you were skelped and chivied out of the kitchen this morning because, being, I am sure, desperately hungry, you helped yourself to,

say, a piece of sausage. I am a Wee Poor Thing, too, because—
because—because—"

Unable to name her malady, Twopence rolled over and lay flat
on her back.

"I wish I were Penny," she said, but not aloud. And something
began to swell and ache behind her eyes. It wasn't pretending—
she was a Wee Poor Thing, and she didn't want to be. She
remembered Penny going quietly to her place among the smiling
girls in the back row. If only she hadn't been so angry with
Miss Blencowe—. Why had she been? After all, it was a toss-up
whether she had said "Theodora" or "Twopence"—and, when
requested, she might easily have substituted her baptismal for
her pet name, as Penelope had done. Why hadn't she? Because
of Miss Blencowe's voice and her pen-painted tie? A lot had
happened because of a voice and a pen-painted tie—

Crash!

The noise of a fall—the fall of someone grown-up in the
dry bracken, and a sharp short ejaculation with which, had
she had time to reflect on its purport, Twopence might have
sympathized. But she did not wait to reflect—she ran quickly
through the spinney to the place from which she thought the
sound had come, while Peter Leathery-Ear took himself off in
the opposite direction.

"*Oh!*" she said, in a voice which sympathy made as sweet as
Penelope's. "Oh, *have* you hurt yourself?"

The man who was crawling through the smashed bracken to
get his crutch looked surprised, and a whimsical smile lighted up
his pale, rather moody face.

"Not at all, thank you," he returned.

"I'll get that," and Twopence plunged across to his side and
picked up the crutch. "Now let me help you. I can—I'm strong.
Just try me. You'll see."

"I can manage all right, thanks very much," he said, struggling to his feet with the help of the crutch, while Twopence stood with arms outstretched, as if to catch him and prop him up should he fall again. Finding this was not demanded of her, she picked a trail of bramble from his coat-sleeve, and brushed him down with much solicitude.

"Now you'll do fine," she said, in the idiom of Kirstie, the housekeeper at Tigh-na-Mara.

"I think so," he agreed. "It's really very lucky for a smashed-up chap like me to meet a lady-errant in the woods."

Twopence was not sure of the compliment, but she liked the laugh in his sad voice, and she smiled up at him confidently.

"Shall I help you home?"

"I shall be very glad if you will walk with me, but I can easily hop along by myself, thank you," he said.

"Oh, there are your sketching things!" she cried, pouncing on a little book and a folded camp-stool. "Had you forgotten you had dropped them?"

"No, but I knew it would be unnecessary to tell you," he said, with a grave courtesy which delighted her.

"I think I'll carry these for you," she said. "I think you must have fallen because you had too much to carry, for an invalid."

"Just to the edge of the spinney, please," he said. "But I'm hardly an invalid, and shan't even be suspected of it when my perfectly good new limb arrives next week."

"That will be lovely," said Twopence, walking slowly at his side, and wondering if it hurt his shoulder to be humped up by that long crutch every time he swung along a step. She knew he must have been a soldier, and longed to ask him how he had lost his leg, but somehow she could not.

"He's a grown-up man," she thought. "He'll tell me himself if he wants to."

He seemed curious about her.

"Do you come from Queen Æthelfleda's?" he asked.

"Yes," said Twopence. "But I am spending a day out in the country."

"That is very nice," he said, without surprise. "My sister went to Queen Fleda's. It's a great place."

Twopence began to think she had better leave him.

"I must go now," she said, as they reached the end of the spinney. "That is, if you can manage by yourself."

"Perfectly, thank you. I live only a little way down that lane. If you will come in, my aunt will be delighted to give you tea."

Twopence smiled. It seemed odd for a grown-up man to have an aunt.

"I'm afraid I can't to-day," she said.

"We may meet again. What is your name?"

"Theodora," said Twopence. "Theodora Wood."

"That's a beautiful name. Good-bye."

Twopence felt suddenly lonely as she watched him go. Peter Leathery-Ear had gone too, and it would soon be evening and the night. She was not afraid of the dark, and she had slept many a night on the heather, wrapped in a plaid—but her stepfather had been there too, and it would be rather lonely in this wood, and there was nothing which tempted one to lie down as heather does. She had better climb a tree—not that it would be possible to sleep up a tree, but it would be a satisfactory way of passing the time and reconciling herself to circumstances.

"I'm sorry for that wounded knight," she thought. "He's a Wee Poor Thing too. What lots of them there are, for such different reasons!"

She turned towards the pine trees, unsuspicious of what was in the mind of the "wounded knight" as he hopped along the lane.

"Run away, I'll wager," he thought. "Poor little beggar—kind little beggar, too. Now, I'll have to do something about it. And what? One's always having to do something about something."

His reflections on this trying and certain truth were interrupted by the sight of another little female figure walking lightly and easily up the hilly lane towards the spinney, gay as a daffodil with her bright hair and yellow cap. He stopped as she approached him, but he did not question her, for directly her eyes fell on his sketch-book she stopped too, and spoke to him.

"May I ask you something, sir?" she said, with pretty courtesy. "Are you an artist?"

"I paint," he answered.

"Have you any magilp in the house?"

"I paint in water-colour," he said gravely. "But," he hastened to add "there *is* varnish in the house."

"Father always had magilp in his studio. Will you do me a very great favour?"

"Most gladly."

"It is to varnish this," and Penelope produced the shield. "When I saw you were an artist I thought, 'Magilp would do it.' But I don't *know*. And it would be a great benefit if you would paint the four names on the other side; only—only be sure not to put 'Twopence' Wood. It's Theodora Wood. T-h-e-o-d-o-r-a."

"I see. Yes, I think I can promise to put this job through for you."

"You are very kind!" exclaimed Penelope. "You have no idea how very kind you are being! May I put it in your coat-pocket?"

"Please. And, by the way, have you lost Theodora?"

"Oh, I have, I have!" cried Penelope. "I think I will find her, but it may take time."

"If you go up through the spinney to that clump of pines I think you'll find her," he said. "And then you're going back to Queen Fleda's?"

"Yes, oh yes. I hope we'll be back in time for tea."

"So do I," he agreed, and felt relieved as he hobbled on, while Penelope dashed up the slope into the spinney.

She did not call her sister. If Twopence were to be coaxed out of some hiding-place, there was a better way than that. Directly she reached the pines she slackened her pace, and, having glanced round and seen no one, began to sing in a funny little voice, to the Shean Trews tune that she and her twin always found irresistible:

> "Jocky birdie laid an egg,
> On the window it was laid,
> For my supper it was made,
> Dance, Jocky birdie."

She sang it twice, the second time more loudly and drolly than the first. Then she was rewarded by hearing a chuckle from the branches of the pine, and a minute later Twopence descended, as lightly and speedily as a monkey, finding foothold where it seemed impossible that it should be.

"Och, Twopence," said Penelope, in Kirsty's voice. "Is there nae more sense tae ye than tae get galumphin' oop an' down the fir trees? See the condition ye'll be in."

"Och, Penny, haud yer clash!" returned Twopence, clasping her sister's hand, while her heart swelled as if to bursting-point. "Och, Penelope, I'm wearying to be at hame—"

Penelope squeezed the resin-sticky hand, while she felt remorsefully that for once she had done the wrong thing—that broad Scotch accent had been a mistake. She had meant to make Twopence laugh, as she often had done by her mimicry, but it seemed as if Twopence were going to cry.

"Cheer up, dear," she whispered. "Soon we'll be going North again, and it'll seem all the bonnier because we haven't seen anything like it for so long."

Twopence stared angrily at her twin, while a dirty tear rolled down one cheek. Penelope knew the reason of that furious look, and forbore to notice the visible sign of the weakness of grief.

"I've missed you dreadfully," she said, "and I'm awfully glad I've found you. The two girls in our dorm. are nice. You'll like them."

"I shan't. I shall hate them."

"Och, Twopence! You should hear Lynette! She'll say to you: 'I'b Lydedde Badderig. Is your dabe Tubbeds? Id's a codspiracy.'"

Twopence refused to smile.

"I've led her a haggerchief," went on Penelope, with an admirably faked sneeze. "I'b sorry for her—it's bidiful to suffer frob thiggs thad sound fuddy ad are agody."

"Och, shut up, Penny!" cried Twopence. "I can't think how you do those sneezes," she went on admiringly, "when you haven't really a cold at all."

"A gift," said Penelope, resuming her normal voice and bearing. "Twopence, it's terribly nice to have found you again."

Suddenly Twopence clasped her twin round the waist. It *was* nice—Penelope was better than the Wee Poor Things, though she loved them too. Penelope was a darling—she would go back with her. There would be tremendous misery to face, but Penelope would be there, and somehow things would come all right.

CHAPTER IV

Reprimanded

THE twins, as Penelope had hoped, reached Queen Æthelfleda's in time for tea. But their pleasure at this act was modified when Matron, with unsmiling eyes, informed them that they were not to enter the bright dining-hall, from which came an appetizing smell of hot toast and a gay sound of laughter and voices, but must go straight to Miss Armstrong's study. They had not yet heard the head-mistress's voice, though on the previous night they had seen her dignified figure pass the open door of the hall while they were having tea, and had been a little awed by the swish of her grey silk dress. Maynie's dresses had swished, but not in quite the same way. Twopence had at once decided that she disliked the tall, uninterested lady, and Penelope, instinctively realizing that here was a new kind of force to be dealt with, was unusually doubtful as to how she would tackle it. Hand-in-hand, according to the childhood habit of which they never thought of ridding themselves, they went soberly down the long polished corridor, which smelt cold, and paused outside the door to which they had been directed. Twopence was about to turn the handle, but Penelope, remembering the prefects' study, restrained her.

"You always knock at doors here," she said in a low voice.

Twopence stared.

"Like a servant?" she questioned.

Penelope gave her a soothing look.

"No—it is just done," she said, and, screwing up her little sunburnt hand, gently rapped on one of the black panels. Her nose wrinkled up as she did so—to the end of her life Penelope couldn't bear the sensation of knocking at a door. Neither could Twopence, but for a different reason.

There was the swish of the grey silk dress, and the door opened, softly and purposefully. The twins gazed up at the tall person confronting them. They were frightened, but they had a way of looking at what made them afraid—for a minute, anyhow.

"Come in, Theodora," said a deep, grave voice. "Penelope, you will remain outside for the present."

So this time Twopence was to come in and Penelope to stay out—and it did not seem as if Twopence stood to gain by the reverse of her fortunes.

For what seemed two hours, and was in reality perhaps ten minutes, Penelope waited, throned in lonely magnificence on a golden-plush chesterfield which spread inviting arms at the end of the corridor, presenting in its solid luxury an ironic contrast with the nervous discomfort of the succession of the guilty or scared to whom it had offered hospitality. She felt cold, hungry and miserable when the door opened, in the same restrained and yet forceful manner, and a small figure slunk out, its head determinedly averted and its shoulders shaking as with paroxysms of laughter or sobs. Penelope slid to her feet and, forgetting Miss Armstrong, stared in consternation after her retreating sister.

Twopence was crying. An unspoken code of honour forbade one sister to comment on the grief of the other—especially if the other happened to be Twopence. What had been said or done to her to make her cry? She hadn't cried like that since the puppy died, nearly two years ago. Penelope watched her as she blundered slowly along. There was a big hole in her stocking, showing just above the back of her brogue. Half-way down the corridor she stopped stupidly, and rubbed her sleeve over her eyes with the gesture of a boy. And she gave out a dreadful snuffling and choking sound—oh! it was awful when it was as bad as that, and simply couldn't be held in! Penelope's little white teeth closed on her lower lip, and she clenched her hands. The half-shy, friendly, charming look vanished from her face—for a moment she was very like the Twopence who had stood alone outside the Lower Third form-room that morning.

"Go in, please."

The grey-silk presence was before, above her, and she was not afraid. She looked up with blazing eyes.

"Oh, how unhappy Twopence is!"

It was a genuine cry of the heart. Miss Blencowe would not have recognized it, but Miss Armstrong did, though Penelope did not guess it.

"Your sister Theodora is a very spoilt little girl," she said. "She will not always be unhappy, I hope."

Penelope looked in surprise at Miss Armstrong, whom she had followed into a warm and flowery room. Twopence spoilt! How could she be? Who had spoilt her? Tommy Merton, in one of Father's father's old books, was a spoilt child—Twopence wasn't a bit like him. With her surprise her charm came back to her little face, pale against her bracken-gold hair, and Miss Armstrong's eyes softened. This twin was unlike the child who, suddenly stubborn and angry with the memories of the morning, had faced her a quarter of an hour ago, though outside the door she had looked very much the same. It would be possible to deal with her more gently.

"I wonder if you realize," she said, in the voice which made Penelope feel small and solemn and afraid, "that you did a very serious thing when you went alone out of school this afternoon?"

Faced with this question, Twopence would have been argumentative; Penelope merely explained.

"I went to find Twopence—Theodora," she said gently, as

if hoping that would make everything all right. "I began to be anxious about her, and I thought I could find her."

"It was natural that you should be alarmed about your sister. You should have told one of the mistresses where you thought she would be. Have you read the rules of the school?"

"No," said Penelope, apologetically.

"To-morrow you will hear them read in the hall. Remember that when you are older you will understand; at present it is your duty to obey."

"Yes," whispered Penelope. She was willing to obey, to do anything the grey-silk lady liked, if she only knew what it was. It was generally quite easy to do what people liked.

"One of the most important," said Miss Armstrong, "is that no girl may go without school-bounds alone."

Penelope gasped. Freedom was in her bones—she loved space and felt the necessity of occasional solitude almost as much as did Twopence.

"Never—go—out—alone!" she exclaimed.

Miss Armstrong glanced at her sharply.

"*Never*," she repeated. "Do you quite understand?"

Penelope shook her head.

"No," she said; "but perhaps I will when I'm older. … Just now," she added dreamily, "I must obey."

Miss Armstrong gave her another quick glance. She had not expected this repetition of her own axiom, and she wondered why she had asked Penelope if she quite understood. She saw that the child was not resentful, was not posing, was simply stating to herself a fact of fate, and was preparing to make the best of it. Thoughts were chasing one another through Penelope's brain. It would be quite pleasant to go into the woods with Archie and Lynette, even if Miss Blencowe were somewhere at the back— she pictured Miss Blencowe as somewhere at the back—she might coax Twopence to share this point of view; they would play those unknown games, hockey and cricket, on a piece of green grass; she could see the trees from the windows. She sighed a little sigh, half of a resignation which had nothing martyr-like. The head-mistress was satisfied—not because of what Penelope had said or sighed, but because of some inexplicable quality in her. She did not believe in petting her pupils, but Penelope was not only a pupil—she was Penelope.

"Yes, you must," she said, and her voice was not frightening any more. "Don't think you'll be unhappy, dear. You will find there are lots of things at Queen Æthelfleda's which will make you very happy, so that you will forget that any rule which once seemed tiresome even exists. Now go and have some tea with your sister."

Penelope looked at her in gratitude for the kindness of her voice, and, with a smile, softly left the room from which the crying Twopence had stumbled a quarter of an hour before.

Miss Armstrong was neither cruel nor terrifying. The day would end quite happily after all—if only Twopence were not so miserable.

Penelope's face saddened again. Things had straightened themselves for her now, but she knew that they were still very crooked for Twopence.

CHAPTER V

More Trouble

PENELOPE was right. Things were still much agley for her twin. Twopence bitterly resented the fate that had decreed that she should cry before Miss Armstrong. Against the head-mistress she felt no grievance—she was quite a different person from Miss Blencowe, and though her wrath might be terrible, it was not irritating. It was obviously just—there was some quality about her that made it likely that she was right when she called running away from school dishonourable. In her heart Twopence knew that she was really not dishonourable—only the circumstances of this new and hateful life had enraged her and might have made her so—she knew that she might be anything in one of her blind fits of passion. A week ago there had been every chance that school might be a success—or that Twopence might be a success at school, which meant the same—now the usual thing, the old miserable thing that belonged to home in Scotland, and that she could even remember as belonging to home in Italy, had happened: she was shut out, alone, but for Penelope—and Penelope was in.

In wretched silence she had undressed that night, only half hearing the excited friendly chatter of Archie and Lynette, who occasionally stole curious looks at her, as if they would have been willing to include her in the conversation, but waited for Penelope to give them the signal. And Penelope, fearing lest Twopence should resent intrusion on her grief, did not give it.

The next day began with the promise of better things, as

next days always do. Ensconced in a new desk next her sister, Twopence felt some interest in her possessions: her pencils and pens, the coloured covers of her note-books. Lynette Mannering, the friendliest individual that ever blotted an exercise, showed her a bone pencil-case which, if scrutinized in a lucky light at a lucky angle, disclosed six views of Edinburgh. "I thought they would idderest you, beig frob Scotladd," she said in triumph as Twopence, not having seen one, though she suspected a Holyrood Palace on the right, thanked her in a whisper—the occasion was a grammar lesson—and returned the treasure. Whereupon Miss St. John, who always saw everything, and never pretended she didn't, swooped down on Lynette and confiscated it. It seemed as if even friendliness with Twopence were unlucky. So the outcast felt, though Lyn showed no resentment.

The third day of the term brought fresh troubles.

"I say," remarked Archie as they were dressing in the morning. "I forgot to tell you that you're supposed to wear your hair tied back, in school and at games. Cynthia and Kate were taking notes of the people who hadn't done it at brekker yesterday—there was a Violet, and a Rose, and two Prims. You'd better do it to-day, or there'll be trouble."

"We haven't a ribbon," said Penelope, pausing in the act of brushing her hair, and regarding Archie with anxiety, while Twopence thrust out her chin, an ominous expression which her sister did not notice.

"I'll led you wud," said Lynette. "I owe id you for the haggerchief. By the way, have I gived id bagg to you?"

"There's no hurry," said Penelope politely, and she accepted the rather crumpled ribbon with a grateful smile, and began to strain back her hair.

"Don't do it too tightly," said Archie.

"The idea is that wud should't loog too preddy," said Lyn,

"bud there's no reasod why wud should pull up wud's eyebrows ad give wudself such paidful spasbs."

"I *do* look rather funny, don't I?" said Penelope, interested in a new possibility for her face. And, drawing down her features and thrusting out her lower lip, she hung her head.

"I'm a jug," she explained, relaxing a moment to let herself speak. "A jug hanging on a dresser."

Down went her head again.

"You're a silly ass," said Archie, and there was affectionate envy in her voice.

"Do it again!" begged Lynette, as Penelope recomposed her features and arranged her hair in the new and business-like fashion school demanded.

"Do something else!" said Archie.

"I wish I had a bowler hat!" said Penelope, looking round the dormitory as if the required object might suddenly materialize. "I make a topping hen, but it needs a bowler hat."

"Why?"

"Oh, I don't know—it just does. Wait till you see. ... Oh, I can do a cheese—I'll do that to-night. I'm glad I'm in the Primrose Dorm. The cap is just the right colour for a rather pale cheese."

"I'b glad you're id the Pribrose Dorb too," said Lynette heartily. "Id would have been a swiddle if the Roses or Violets had got you."

Twopence regarded the new Penelope, looking at once younger and older with her hair tied back, and her heart swelled. Neither Archie nor Lynette had offered to lend her a ribbon, and, if she had had one, she did not know how she would tie back her hair—she had a horrible fear that the ends of it would not meet. Yet she must keep the rules—she did not want another interview with Miss Armstrong.

"I say!" she said, and the words came slowly, as if they were very difficult to speak. "I haven't a ribbon—will it matter?"

Penelope's hand went up to her bow, but Lynette sprang forward and opened a drawer.

"It's rather used-looking," she said doubtfully. "Will it do?"

It was very used-looking, but Twopence said it would. There was silence as she gathered her thick, straight short hair into a tuft and, with chin thrust out, wound the ribbon round about it and tied it tightly. The result justified her fears. Her face assumed an expression of startled agony, which Archie and Lynette thought was meant to be funny—Penelope knew better, but she was not in time to restrain a delighted burst of laughter from the deluded ones, who anticipated a "turn" equal in merit to the pretty twin's representation of a jug hanging on the dresser. They were soon to discover their mistake. With scarlet cheeks, and eyes that flamed with anger, Twopence tore off the ribbon and faced round upon them.

"I know I look hideous!" she cried. "I know I *am* hideous. Laugh at me if you like! I don't care! I won't wear a ribbon, though—Cynthia and Kate may say what they like. They can't force me to do it if I won't!"

"Oh, help, help!" moaned Archie, pressing her hand to her forehead and creeping behind Lynette. "Let me take cover behind the sheltering mound."

"Shudub!" advised Lyn, in perfect good humour, while her brown eyes regarded Twopence with curiosity rather than consternation. "I say, Theodora, does id ofden cobe od like thad?"

Twopence flung the ribbon at its donor, who caught it neatly and began to fold it up, still staring with interest at an unusual spectacle at Queen Æthelfleda's—a human being physically shaken and tortured with rage.

Penelope thought it might be time for breakfast. To her relief, Archie and Lynette said no more, and Twopence followed them down the bare polished staircase, ribbonless, but otherwise not to be distinguished in general appearance and bearing from the blue-skirted, white-shirted girls who hurried from every dormitory to the hall where meals were eaten. To her further relief, no comment was made on Twopence, who, as Kirstie would have said, "managed through the forenoon" without any mishap. And, after one o'clock lunch, when everyone ran down to "post-table," where two of the prefects stood handing out the mail, which came late to this country place, she was delighted to see a flat parcel addressed to herself. It must be the shield—the artist who had promised to help her had not forgotten.

"Thank you," she said fervently, as the tall Cynthia handed it to her. And the head girl smiled.

"Chocolates?" she asked sympathetically, and, without waiting for a reply, went on sorting letters, while Archie and Lynette looked enviously at the new-comer on whom Cynthia had smiled and to whom she had addressed a remark.

"Cydthia's sibbly toppig!" sighed Lynette, as they escorted Penelope up to the dormitory, one on either side.

"Don't mutilate her lovely name like that," said Archie, quite crossly. "It isn't for you to speak of her till that cold is better."

"Do you think I shall have time to fix this up before hockey?" inquired Penelope tactfully, as she unwrapped the shield.

"I say! How well they've done it for you! Who did it?" cried Archie.

Penelope assumed a funny look of profound mystery. She had lived long enough in Scotland to know that they are puir feckless buddies wha must aye be for tellin' ilka thing that comes to them. Twopence should know, but Archie and Lynette should just go on wondering.

They did not resent her reticence, but showed great interest and resource in re-fixing the shield—not really a difficult task, as Penelope had providentially forgotten to restore the screw-driver of the Sixth. No sooner had they finished than a whistle shrilled along the corridor.

"That's for the first game," said Archie, hastily removing her skirt and pulling her gym tunic over her head. "You come down on the second whistle, Penny—Kate and I are playing with the beginners then."

"Kate is the captaid of the first, and Archie bay be id the third eleved this year," said Lynette.

"I 'spect I'll be a silly ass!" said Penelope, in that despondent voice that comes so pleasantly to the ears of the initiated.

"You needn't bother about that!" said Lynette, who had wisdom. "It's asses who are the libit. *Silly* asses are sibbly toppig."

"So they are!" agreed Archie. "Come on, Lyn, hustle. Good-bye for just now, Penelope."

Penelope had changed into her tunic, and was strutting up and down with her hands on her hips, loving to feel the free strong movement of her muscles, when the door opened and Twopence came in, with the chastened expression that her sister knew so well as the aftermath of a temper. It was safe and desirable to speak to her now.

"Hallo, Twopence," she said. "We're to be ready for hockey in twenty minutes. You have heaps of time to change."

Twopence again looked dangerous.

"*Hockey!*" she said, contemptuously. "Imagine anyone wasting every afternoon on a stupid game like that!"

She walked to the window and stared across to the hockey-field, whence came sounds of sharp thwacking, shrill whistles, and curt shouted orders.

"It must have something in it when they all like it so," said Penelope. "Look, Twopence. That's Cynthia Waynfleet—by that wooden shed near the tennis-courts; and I think Kate Croydon is with her. Perhaps they aren't playing now because they are to coach us later."

Twopence looked. She thought she knew Cynthia, of whom she had heard the enthusiastic Primroses speak, but she wasn't sure.

"She stands as if she were too lazy to live," she said.

"Oh, no, Twopence. She stands beautifully, though she looks so lazy. I'm sure she isn't really. She is languid, because, Archie says, she has a secret sorrow."

Twopence snorted, examining Cynthia, who was evidently being teased or challenged by the little group of grown-up girls who stood round her. Suddenly she left them, walked lazily across the ash court, and, pausing for a moment, glanced at the net, which was stretched taut, ready for a game. Then she bent a little forward, approached with a light, sure run, and jumped it, easily and beautifully. The girls she had left laughed and clapped, but she did not look back at them, but came towards the school, the tiniest shadow of a smile passing over her face.

"They said she couldn't!" exulted Penelope. "And she did!"

"It isn't very high—a tennis-net," said Twopence, a curious little stir at her heart.

She liked Cynthia for apparently not hearing the applause of her friends, for not looking back, as if she had done her jump to please herself and didn't care what they thought.

"Ah, but she did it well. Come, Twopence, get ready."

Twopence looked doubtfully at Penelope, strange in the tunic that suited her so well, her eyes shining with pleasure. *She* was glad and eager to try this new game; she was not afraid of being unable to understand the directions which that black-browed captain would give so shortly; she was happy—she was "in it." Then her gaze wandered to the door—she had wondered about that shield: who had taken it away, what had been or would be said. She started, rubbed her eyes, went close to make sure. Yes! there was no mistake:

FALCONER, GEORGINA.
MANNERING, LYNETTE M.
WOOD, PENELOPE L.
WOOD, THEODORA.

"Wood, Theodora!" she turned to Penelope, who was looking at her doubtfully but proudly, her cheeks flushed.

"Penny!" she exclaimed at once. "How did you get it done?"

"I took it off the door the first day," explained Penelope. "And I met the artist man you said you saw in the wood—the 'Wounded Knight.' He said he'd make it all right—and there it is, you see ... I didn't tell you before," she hastened to add, "because it would have been such a drop if it hadn't come off."

"Such a drop if it hadn't come off!" Pure Archie Falconer! How did Penelope understand them so easily—catch their way of speaking so quickly?

Twopence stared at the shield. ... Ah, but the "Wood, Twopence" would still be behind the decorous Theodora, burnt in with a red-hot poker, never to be erased or obliterated. A slow, painful red, different from Penelope's bright flush, crept into her cheeks, and trouble grew in her eyes. She had done something that would make Miss Armstrong angry—she knew it would, and Penelope knew too, and had resolved to hide it and save her. She had succeeded—up to a point. But she couldn't succeed altogether.

"Well, you needn't have bothered," she said heavily, "for I shall tell Miss Armstrong that I did it."

Penelope gasped.

"Twopence! Why?"

"I don't know. I shall."

"Twopence, darling, she'll be so furious! It's all right now—it's just as good as ever it was. Oh, Twopence, it has been bad enough—don't get a lot of extra things to make you miserable."

Penelope's voice quivered. One of the things which hurts most is to find that carefully contrived help is useless. She had felt elated that afternoon, after the fixing of the shield—it had counteracted the effect that the unfortunate hair-ribbon episode had had upon her. And now Twopence wouldn't let her triumph succeed—Twopence meant to bring more sorrow and shame upon herself. When she thrust out her chin like that she always kept to what she said she would do. Penelope could have cried.

"You mustn't think I am ungrateful, Penny, darling," said Twopence, whose resolute heart was more touched by the tremble in her sister's voice than she herself knew. "I am not. But—but—but—"

She could not explain.

A sharp whistle sounded from the hockey-field, and was answered by another from the school building.

"That's for us!" cried Penelope. "Come along, Twopence. Come to hockey first. You can tell afterwards."

"No," said Twopence. "I'm going to tell now."

Penelope took her very new hockey-stick and went downstairs and out towards the field with a heavy heart. School was being dreadful for Twopence—far more dreadful than she had thought possible.

It was characteristic that not for a moment did it come into her mind that she, as well as Twopence, might be involved in the trouble that the voluntary confession would bring about. She seldom got into scrapes, people seldom were angry with her, and she did not expect them to be.

"Here's Penny!" cried Archie, leaping down the grassy bank that dipped down from the hockey-ground to the tennis-courts. "Hurrah! Penny, race me along this path. Kate wants to see you run, to guess where to put you for the beginners' game."

Penelope thrilled at the friendly voice, and, casting down her stick, dashed after Archie. She would catch her! It was glorious!

She drank the cold, sunny October air; the blood came into her cheeks, not hotly and uncomfortably, but exultingly, as if to decorate her happiness. She felt as if she had winged heels; she could have run and run, faster, further. The wind flowed back from her like waves from a swimmer, and yet more lightly, more excitingly than heavy, pushing water. Laughing, she leapt past Archie.

A whistle sounded from the bank.

"Get your stick and come up, kiddie!" shouted the black-browed Kate. "Don't burst yourself on the trial trip. We'll put you on the forward line."

CHAPTER VI

A Desperate Act

HALF an hour before the Primroses came up from hockey—time to move. Twopence did not want to see any of them—not even Penelope. In her wretchedness she preferred to be alone.

Her mouth was set straight as she piled her clothes in heaps on the little yellow bed, in which she would not sleep any more, and her hands trembled as she opened the door of her locker and took out the books which had accompanied her on the escapade of three days ago, and a new clean scroll on which was written:

> SOSIETY OF WEE POOR THINGS
> 1. Peter Lethery-Ere
> 2. A Woonded Nite (Hon. Member)
> 3. Benjamin the Beetel.
>   (Sined) 2d. Wood.

She hardly looked at it, but rolled it up and tied it with a piece of ribbon pulled from her best nightgown. Nor did she give a thought to Benjamin, who, emerging from behind the fireplace, had had a terrible effect on Archie and Lynette two mornings ago. She had caught him and put him in a commodious old pencil-box, sympathizing with him because he was obnoxious to the Primroses. Since then she had been troubled about his diet. Her stepfather, who was familiar with every intimate detail about all that runs or flies or crawls or climbs, would know what beetles liked to eat, but she suspected that he would be too much

entertained by Maynie to take the trouble to answer a post card
on the subject. She did not care just now if Peter Leathery-Ear
were chivied from the kitchen every hour of his interesting life,
or if the Wounded Knight fell in the woods and couldn't get
up, or if Benjamin starved. "2d. Wood" was the member of the
society most desirous of sympathy—and "2d. Wood" was too
miserable to give it to herself.

She had expected Miss Armstrong to be angry—but she had
not expected such a punishment as this. Banishment from the
Primrose Dorm—from Penelope! She would hardly see her twin,
except in school, where people did not seem quite real, because
they were occupied with something imposed upon them from
without. She had been shown the room where she was now to
sleep—grey, with a grey check quilt and a black bedstead—a
sombre little place, with a hint of the prison-cell about its
appearance. Perhaps she would be forced to wear a black cap
and a black tie, instead of the gay primrose ones which she and
Penelope loved—everyone would know that she was an outcast.

Yet she was not sorry that she had told. Had she considered
the matter, she probably would not have been sorry that she had
burnt that "Twopence Wood" on the shield which was to inform
future generations of this year's inhabitants of the Primrose
Dorm. She thought it very unlucky that she should have been
in a temper on the first day, just as she would have thought it
unlucky to have had toothache or a pain inside. She just "had"
the affliction, and Penelope hadn't.

She hadn't incriminated Penelope, and her not having done
so was so much a matter of course that she did not congratulate
herself on it. "A kni—an artist I met did it." It was quite true,
and Miss Armstrong accepted it at once. Miss Armstrong
was prepared for any out-of-the-way action on the part of
Theodora Wood. She consoled herself with the thought that the
phenomenon of children with both parents step-parents was not

likely to present itself to her again. Penelope and Theodora had obviously been so much neglected that she felt it her duty, at whatever cost, to keep them with her, when to send them away would mean to return them to the unrestricted life they had led at Tigh-na-Mara. Theodora was the dangerous spirit, and Theodora must be subdued. Isolation would render her safe, harmless, and probably tameable.

She did not guess that this same Theodora was already isolated in that isolation of the spirit that grown-up people learn to bear but that children cannot understand. She did not guess the pride that had led Twopence, accused of being "dishonourable," to her study with her confession, and the overwhelming misery that filled the child's heart as she staggered with her possessions from the Primrose Dorm to the little grey cell which was now to be hers.

At last her task was over. She went sadly to the window where she and Penelope had stood earlier in the afternoon. The girls ran or sauntered from the hockey-field in twos and threes, flushed, laughing and talking. Cynthia Waynfleet and Kate Croydon came first, glancing over a sheet of paper; Penelope, Archie and Lynette lingered near the goalposts—the others showed Penelope how to shoot, and she listened and watched, as interested as she had been when Andrew Dalziel, Kirstie's son, showed her how to reef a mainsail and how to tack before the wind. Twopence thought lovingly of that tiny yacht, as she paid off before the wind, straining to disobey and yet obeying, excitable and lovable as a living thing. She remembered the cut of her prow through the swirling water, and the creak of her sails and of the wings of the gulls that soared and volplaned around her, as if boasting of a trick that she couldn't do. She remembered how once she had dared Penelope to swim from one island to another, and how they had done it, and their stepfather had been angry with her, but not for long. And climbing Cruachan Dhu—the bit where a rope was needed; and skating along that long eastern bay of the loch, which froze so hard and well towards the end of November— these things seemed so real and worth while compared with that stupid, rushing, thwacking game of which they had never heard before school, and which Penelope was settling down to enjoy. And Penelope would enjoy it—as much as, if not more than, the other things. ...

The door was flung sharply open, and Twopence started round from the window. There stood the black-browed Kate, and Cynthia, who languidly leaned against the wall and regarded the room and its one small occupant as if she were thinking of something quite different and far away.

"Why weren't you at hockey, you young slacker?" inquired Kate.

"Had you sick leave?" suggested Cynthia.

Twopence felt the blood rush into her cheeks, and her eyes blazed. She did not say a word.

"And where's your hair-ribbon?" demanded Kate. "And, by the way, ask that sister of yours why she hasn't returned my screw-driver."

"Oh, yes," said Cynthia's lazy voice. "I have a box of books I should quite like to open. Please don't forget to inquire about that screw-driver."

Twopence glanced at the screw-driver lying on the window-seat beside her, where Penelope had flung it after replacing the shield. The fiery feeling she knew and dreaded leapt up into her brain; her heart thumped as if it wanted to get out of her body; she forced her muscles taut lest the trembling of her limbs should betray her agitation. How dare these girls burst into her room—it wasn't hers now, but they did not know that—and question her as if she were a servant and regard her with such scornful eyes? She had not time to reflect, or she would have known that she hated Cynthia's indifferent politeness more than Kate's contempt. The combination of the two maddened her. With a quick, frenzied gesture she seized the screw-driver.

"Here it is!" she cried, and flung it, as if she were hurling a javelin, straight across the room to where they stood.

"Look out!" Cynthia was straight and alive, and quick as flame. She dashed her arm in front of Kate's face, and caught the steel of the tool, holding it in a tight grasp. Then, as she relaxed her grip, and a few drops of blood showed between her thumb and forefinger, she turned suddenly, absurdly white, and the horrified child standing by the window saw her collapse as if all her sinews had turned to cotton, and sway forward. ...

"Hold on, Cynthia!" cried Kate, her arms around her. "Hold on! You aren't hurt! It's all right!"

That was Kate's formula, well known to all at Queen Fleda's, applied to every woe that schoolgirl may suffer, from a black eye inflicted by a cricket-ball to a black star conferred as order of disgrace by a form-mistress. Never did she lose confidence in its cheering properties, though often, as now, it seemed inaudible to the person it was intended to benefit.

"All ri'—" droned Cynthia's voice. "Lemme lie flat—it's a' ri'—"

Kate obediently put her flat on her back.

"Get some water, you little blighter!" she commanded Twopence, who stood perfectly still, overcome by a sensation she had never before experienced. "And tell the rest of your lot to go and wash—they can't come in here and make a crowd."

Twopence rushed to obey, but when she came back Cynthia was again standing by the door, as she had been when she asked about the screw-driver, only very, very pale. To Twopence, who had never before seen anyone faint, this pallor was as dreadful as that of death itself.

"Kate, *don't*," she was saying. "*Please* don't. You make me feel such a miserable ass."

Her voice was quivering, as if she were disappointed about something, and Kate was holding her by the arm. Twopence suddenly realized that, though Kate looked so fierce, and talked so definitely, she would do, or refrain from doing, anything in the world at Cynthia's will.

"Don't worry yourself, old thing," she said in a surprisingly gentle voice. "Only I think that wretched kid ought to be brought to her senses. She deserves a good fright. She can't go on like this, you know."

"Oh, I'll see about her coming to hockey," said Cynthia, a little impatiently. "Only let this drop, Kate."

"Oh, *there* you are!" exclaimed Kate, turning suddenly on Twopence, who stood waiting with the glass of water. "Take that away. And I suppose you have sufficient instinct for your own self-preservation to hold your miserable tongue about what you have done."

"Report yourself at study number one after tea," said Cynthia in her normal lazy voice. "In a hair-ribbon, please."

CHAPTER VII

In Which Twopence Makes a Resolution

TWOPENCE did not look at Penelope during a tea which, for her, was the more dismal because the other girls, hungry and lively after a long afternoon of games or gardening, seemed to enjoy it so much. When it was over she joined the others for evening prep., which she was too unhappy to do well or badly, and as the clock struck eight, and they crowded round the fire for half an hour of talk and hard biscuits before bed, she went slowly up to her little grey room to prepare herself for the ordeal of Cynthia Waynfleet.

She did not know how to comfort herself. Angry she had often been, or miserable, or, in spite of Penelope, lonely, but shame was a new and overpoweringly wretched sensation. She would have given everything she had to have been able to cancel the later part of that afternoon. What was it that had made her throw that screw-driver at Cynthia and Kate? She had never thought she might do a thing to hurt anyone—it was wrong, perhaps the wrongest thing in the world, and it had made her hateful.

She seemed to herself to be only half alive as she hunted through her possessions for a piece of string, and, straining back her hair, tied it into position with a tight knot. She wondered what would happen to her—if she would always be like this, wrong in a world which suddenly seemed to her right.

Quietly she left her room and went to the end of the corridor, where, next the door labelled "Prefects," was one inscribed "Head Girl," and bearing a narrow frame of brass, which contained a card on which was printed in Early English letters what Archie had called "her lovely name," Cynthia Waynfleet.

Twopence had put her hand on the knob when she remembered that Penelope had said, "You always knock at doors here." She hastily did what was right, and, in answer to the "Come in," which didn't seem to care if the person outside came or not, crept upon the scene of further disgrace.

Cynthia sat at her writing-table, a pen in her hand, an exercise book open before her. For a minute she stared at Twopence, as if she had forgotten who she was and why she had come, then she said, wearily and courteously:

"Sit down a minute, will you? I want to finish this while I feel inclined to do it."

Seeing an unassuming and hard three-legged stool by the fire, Twopence cautiously placed herself upon it, and while Cynthia wrote on with hardly a pause, she glanced about the room. She was not in a mood to see much, and there was not much to see, but she was conscious of the gaiety and goldenness of a bowl of late nasturtiums, and the lovely shape of their shadows on the bare wall against which they stood, of a low case full of books which looked as if they had been used constantly and arranged with care, and of three black and white photographs, framed in passepartout, which hung in a straight line by the side of the fireplace, level with her eyes as she sat. All three were signed— one "Timmy," one "Pamela," and one "Uf-uf." "Timmy" was like Cynthia, turned into a boy and wearing a blazer; "Pamela" was like Cynthia, with darker hair and a more erect head, and those eyes which look as if their owner were ready to do any difficult thing anyone likes to ask; "Uf-uf" was in khaki, and it was at "Uf-uf" that Twopence stared, with amazement and interest which, for the moment, overcame her misery. For this "Uf-uf," though he looked younger and happier, was very much like—in fact he *must* be, he *was* the "Wounded Knight" whom she had helped, and who had helped Penelope, in the coppice with the pines.

She started as Cynthia suddenly wheeled round in her revolving chair, and regarded her.

"Oh—yes," she said. "Theodora Wood."

She paused, looking at Twopence as if she were still trying to remember. Her long hand, whose fingers still held her pen, lay on the writing-table.

"Oh—yes," said Cynthia again. "It was hockey, wasn't it? All the girls in your year are supposed to play games every afternoon, unless they have medical certificates. You haven't one, I suppose?"

Twopence shook her head.

"Well, be down on the field by three o'clock to-morrow. Your sister will show you. She was there to-day."

She turned as if that were all, and then wheeled round again.

"By the way, I must enter some excuse for to-day!"

"I partly didn't want to play," said Twopence, "and I *was* partly seeing Miss Armstrong."

Cynthia's eyebrows went up. She opened a big flat book, found the name "Theodora Wood," and neatly entered by the side of it—"Sept. 25th — Miss Armstrong."

"Be there to-morrow," she said, shutting the book and turning to her work again.

Twopence knew she was dismissed. And Cynthia had said nothing, nothing of the miserable, inexplicable episode of the afternoon. It would have been better if she had, if she had been reproachful or angry, if she had inflicted some punishment. As it was, Twopence knew herself plunged into lower depths than those of disgrace—the depths of the people who simply cannot be counted. Cynthia, in accordance with the duties of her office, had investigated the defection with regard to hockey—the insult to herself she was too proud, too indifferent, to remark upon. Twopence felt again the little stir that had come to her heart when the challenged Cynthia had jumped the tennis-net and walked on without turning to find out if her friends had seen her. It was excited by a quality she hadn't noticed before in any of her friends or acquaintances, and which she admired with something deep down in her, strange and troubling, something that made her long, for the first time in her life, to say she was sorry.

She got as far as the door, opened it, shut it again, turned back, and went softly towards Cynthia's chair. Cynthia started, and looked at her questioningly.

"That is all," she said.

"No," said Twopence, in a low voice, which she seemed to hear speaking outside herself, like someone else's. "I wish to say I am very sorry—for hurting you this afternoon."

The deep flush which she felt like a pain crept gradually up her cheeks, but she kept her eyes fixed upon Cynthia's, until suddenly red-hot irons seemed to rush into them, and she knew she might cry. Quickly she lowered them, and, setting her teeth into her lower lip, made a valiant effort to control the waggling of her chin.

"You needn't apologize for hurting me," said Cynthia's voice, no longer bored, but sweet and friendly. "You did not hurt much. See—" And she opened her hand, where a tiny jagged scar showed between the thumb and first finger.

Twopence fought to push down the emotions that surged up in her, shaking and hurting her as much as her tempers did.

She could neither speak nor move. Cynthia opened her mouth to say something, but, seeing how things were, shut it again, until, with a little shake of her shoulders, Twopence looked up.

"It made you faint," she whispered.

Cynthia flushed.

"*That* was nothing," she said sharply. "*That* did not mean I was hurt."

Twopence looked at her quickly. She seemed angry, and her

anger was somehow a relief, a tonic, it helped more than anything else could have done to keep back those horrible tears.

"I would have given anything not to have done it," she said, and, though her voice was very low, Cynthia could hear the sincerity of it. "I do not think I shall ever get into a temper again."

"Don't," said Cynthia. And then, hastily, as if ashamed of the feeling she had put into the monosyllable—"Bad temper makes people so dreadful, doesn't it? It's such a miserable business. I don't know. Perhaps you were miserable yourself. What was the matter?"

Twopence shook her head.

"Everything has gone wrong to-day," she said unsteadily. "Since the hair-ribbon—they laughed at me when I put mine on. They laughed at Penny too, and she pretended to be a jug, and she said she'd be a hen and a cheese afterwards, and they liked her awfully."

Cynthia might have looked puzzled, but, being head girl, she did not.

"If they laughed at Penelope and she didn't mind," she said, "why did you mind so much when they laughed at you?"

"Penny can stop being funny and just be pretty and nice," said Twopence heavily. "It isn't Penny they laugh at, it's something she puts on. But when they laugh at me, I can't stop what they laugh at. It's quite different."

Cynthia saw that it was. She stretched out her hand and removed the piece of string. The short thick hair started out again and spread itself round the little face, strangely set and passionate for a child's. The head girl smiled.

"It's very fashionable nowadays to wear one's hair bobbed, and the ribbon rule will need modifying before long," she said. "I don't think you need wear one, meantime. And try to be happy. There's no reason why you shouldn't be."

"I shall try very hard," said Twopence. "But I have tried before, and it has been no good," she added honestly. And her lip quivered.

Cynthia suddenly knew Twopence. She looked at her gently and pitifully.

"You can do anything by trying," she said in a low voice. "I know you can."

Twopence regarded her with questioning and surprised eyes, eyes that said, "How do you know?"

"I have never had a *very* bad temper," said Cynthia, in the slow way that Twopence knew meant it was difficult to say things. "But I am rather a coward—"

"*You?*"

"Yes. In fact, I'm a tremendous coward. You know that—you saw how I fainted to-day because a tiny little drop of blood came out of my hand. When I came to school, I was afraid of everything except water. I hated balance-walking and climbing, for fear I should get giddy; was afraid to jump in case I should fall; I daren't play hockey lest the ball or a stick should hit me and hurt me; I could hardly stand still when I saw someone ready to serve at tennis. And because I was so frightened I was sometimes cross."

Twopence stared in astonishment. It was a new idea to her that people like Cynthia might be afraid of things.

"What made you stop being frightened?" she asked.

Cynthia shook her head.

"I don't know," she said simply. "The feeling just began to go."

"The red-hot feeling?" cried Twopence, wondering if it might be like that. "Little spikes at your finger-ends and behind your knees?"

"Yes, rather like that. I thought it had quite gone, but it hasn't, quite."

Twopence remembered that sudden whiteness and stagger, that "Don't! You'll make me feel such a miserable ass!" Suddenly she understood the anger and disappointment in Cynthia's voice when Kate tried to comfort her.

"And you did all the things you hated?" she asked.

Cynthia nodded. "Except once or twice; and the feeling went—nearly went, I mean."

Twopence stretched out her hand, and, with a rare gesture of affection, laid it on Cynthia's arm.

"I will do all the things I hate," she said quietly, making a vow to herself. "I will do sums and grammar for Miss Blencowe, I will learn to spell. I will play hockey; I will do everything I am asked to do."

"Will you?" said Cynthia, half quizzically.

Twopence looked at her steadily.

"You shall see!" she said. "I knew inside before that I wouldn't, not for long. Now I know I will."

"Good-night," said Cynthia, giving the hand a little shake. "Good luck."

Twopence went softly to her grey room, and, slipping out of her clothes, put on her dressing-gown to wait her turn for a bath. She did not mind waiting now, though she had hated it on other nights. Her grey room was not so bad—her temper, which had always made her unhappy, was not so bad. It would go—Cynthia thought it would.

And this time last night she hadn't known there was a person like Cynthia in the world! All loved and therefore lucky people had seemed like Penelope—happy and good because they were made that way. Cynthia was different.

Twopence, hugging her knees, and glancing round the room, saw the scroll of the Wee Poor Things lying on the bed, where she had cast it after what Kirstie would have called her "flittin'."

"Cynthia was a Wee Poor Thing too," she thought with sympathy. "What lots of them there are!"

Barefoot, she crossed to her locker, and, taking her Indian ink, opened the scroll. Very carefully, in her best printing, under the name of Benjamin the Beetle, she recorded:

"4. Cynthia Waynfleet. Honorary and very Honourable Member."

CHAPTER VIII

Twopence and her Pets

THE next morning has a way of lessening whatever one may have felt the evening before—whether it was a happy or unhappy thing. Although Twopence awoke with the inspiriting remembrance of Cynthia and the vow she had taken in Cynthia's presence, she was also conscious of the loneliness of her little bare room, and of what she called the "punishing look" of the black iron bed and the strip of dark carpet. She thought of Penelope dressing with Archie and Lynette, being funny and happy, as Penelope always was first thing in the morning, and of the three becoming more and more friendly. They might include her in their little clique, but it was unlikely that she would be counted as a Primrose now.

As she soberly brushed and combed her hair, hardly comforted by the remembrance that she need not tie it back, she heard a prolonged "Me-ow-ow-ow," and, a moment later, a familiar black form leapt on to her window-sill, and rubbed its head ingratiatingly against the windowpanes.

"Peter Leathery-Ear! My poor wee thing!" And Twopence rushed to open the window, and, lifting the disreputable black beggar into her arms, kissed him again and again, delighted with the loud rattling purr that came from the depths of his asthmatical chest.

"He's hungry!" she thought despairingly. "And I've nothing to give him—nothing."

Leaning from her window, she saw that Peter had approached her room by a pear espalier with thick branches, which did not extend as far as the Rose, Violet, and Primrose dormitories, but made descent into the garden from hers possible and even easy for a sure-footed person.

"A ridiculous place to put a criminal in!" she thought scornfully. "If I wanted to run away from school in the night I could soon do it." And, as she examined the steps by which she might climb down, she honestly felt it was rather a pity she didn't intend to do it, the opportunity seemed so good a one to be wasted.

"I'm very very sorry your breakfast isn't ready, Peter," she said. "If you could call in in another half hour—could you, do you think?"

Peter reflectively blinked his amber eyes, as if he thought he might, and Twopence, having, with complete indifference as to consequences, ensconced him on the pillow of her bed, took a small cardboard box which had once held india-rubber, and hurried down to breakfast, much cheered by his visit.

What luck! Fish rissoles! It would not be difficult to secrete hers for Peter, especially at the table where the Primroses, Violets, and Roses sat, talking so much that there would not be time for them to notice a sleight-of-hand trick by the outcast from the Grey Dorm. With an eye fixed on Miss Blencowe, who, sitting at the top of the table, was describing the quite obvious weather to a politely attentive Rose, Twopence swept the rissole from her plate, and, as she heard it softly thud into the cardboard box, she could have laughed aloud in triumph. There was no one on her left, Penelope, on her right, did not matter.

So Peter Leathery-Ear had his breakfast, and Benjamin accepted a few crumbs experimentally offered him. Twopence was cheered by this success. She loved to feel that someone wanted her and was dependent on her—Peter's hunger, and the affection he showed after a meal, made her sure of him, and, though Benjamin didn't know it, she told herself that he was far happier safely cloistered in his pencil-box than he would have been had he been allowed to risk his life in a larger area.

She knew her luck with people better than to expect that, because she had promised Cynthia to "try and be happy," she would at once establish a relationship with them as satisfactory as that with the Wee Poor Things. Nor did the results of that day, nor of many others, contradict expectations. Penelope had stepped into her little kingdom; Twopence had missed her chance, and it did not come again easily. She found school work difficult; she simply could not spell, and the terminology of grammar and the processes of arithmetic were so distasteful to her that it was only by a tremendous mental effort that she could fasten her mind upon them, and then, before she had realized it, it was off again, and she was drawing pictures in the margin of a text-book, or dreaming of the loch at home, the spinney where she had spent the day with Peter and met the Wounded Knight, Cynthia in her room with the shadows of flowers on the wall. Miss Blencowe, her opinion strengthened by her memory of that first encounter, thought her obstinate and lazy, a contrast in every way with her sister, who, though handicapped by lack of previous instruction in examination subjects, was eager and interested, regarding sums and analysis as queer puzzles, which perhaps she would not have bothered to work out had she been left to herself, but which she was quite willing to undertake to amuse a mistress. Games were no better. Twopence had stronger muscles than Penelope, and she could run almost as fast, but hockey bored her, and she constantly forgot instructions, exciting the just anger of Kate and the surprised contempt of the others, who loved the game and could not understand anyone who just tolerated it. "Rabbits!" Twopence would think. "Sheep! They like it just because they know they ought to—they think it a 'sporting' thing to do." This and similar reflections consoled her when, after a sharp rebuke, she wrestled with the fury that strove to overcome her. She had vowed before Cynthia to do the thing she hated—and, however frequent her lapses might be, she meant to keep her vow.

She was strengthened by the hope of serving Cynthia. In the brown paper book she had now made—the Book of the Wee Poor Things—she longed for a closely-written record of how she had done this. Everyone else had been helped. On the first page she liked to see the strip of white paper, neatly pasted on to the brown, and bearing the information:

1. Peter Lethery-Ear.

His sine.

Hes a wee poor thing becaws someone has eaten his ear, and he is thin and Most Dejekted in his ribs.

I will give him out of kindness:

(1) Fish, baken, or other sollid foods in the morning, and a drink of cristall water in the sope dysh.

(2) A pat and a kiss on his good ear, and a tikkle under his chinn.

This has been done and is still to be done.

On the second page came:

2. Benjamin the Beetel.

His sine.

Hes a wee poor thing becaws in their craven fere the Primmroses of the P. Dorm would have stampped on him, and he is the foe tho innosent of all wommen.

I will give him out of kindness:

(1) An ellegant home in which to reside free of all rente and charge.

(2) Crumms ad libb when they may be obtayned.

(3) A hansome toom when he shall dye.

This has been done eggscept for (3), which shall bee dewly done, woe worth the day.

On the third:

3. A woonded Nite.

His sine.

Hes a wee poor thing becaws he has had a leg taken away, and consekwently may fall down at any time.

I will give him out of kindness:

The help of my strong rite arm when he shall it requyre.

This has wunce been done, and it will be done agayne, if I meat him, as I sinseerly hope I may.

And on the fourth:

4. Cynthia Waynfleet.

Head Girl of Queen Æthelfleda's.

A Very Honourable Member.

Her sine.

Shes a wee poor thing becaws she has noan dredful fere, and becaws I have herde it said that she has some Secret Sorrow.

I will give her out of kindness and my grateful sole:

Whatever I can but I know not what it may be.

That was the worst of it—if only she knew what it might be!

There were little chances, but in these Twopence was unlucky. One low-clouded November afternoon, as the twins and Archie walked slowly together from the hockey-field, they saw Cynthia and Kate playing singles on the far ash court. Penelope at once skipped with excitement, for she loved to watch these two— Twopence, who remembered what Cynthia had told her about her first sensations at tennis, and who would not own to her sister that she had more than ordinary interest in the head girl, walked rather more soberly than before. But she started as Cynthia missed one of Kate's smashing serves, and the ball sped down towards them. "Get it! Pick it up! Hurry!" said something inside her brain, and it spoke to Penelope too, and more quickly. In an instant Penelope's foot had stopped the ball, and Penelope had flung it up to be caught by Kate, and, rushing to the court, had said she would field till tea-time. And she had fagged balls for Cynthia, while Archie, never scornful of the next best thing, had established herself near Kate's court. Twopence, sore with the realization of a good opportunity lost, walked sadly back to the school building. She felt no resentment towards Penelope—it was always like that, and Penelope did not know that she was longing to do something for Cynthia. However, when her sister, scarlet with exertion, her hair dampened into little rings with the afternoon mist, appeared in her Grey Dorm, she looked up rather crossly.

"Twopence, Cynthia wants you to field balls when she's playing tennis to-morrow," said Penelope doubtfully. She thought Twopence might offer some violent objection.

"Oh, *does* she?" said Twopence.

"Yes. You will, won't you?"

"You didn't say I wouldn't?" Twopence, in sudden alarm, faced round upon her sister.

"No, but I thought you might be bored. Oh—and, Twopence—"

"Well?"

"Archie Falconer has asked us to spend the half-term week-end with her."

Twopence showed some signs of gratification.

"Me too?"

"Of course. And, Twopence, the topping thing about it is that the Falconers live at Morecott Marsh, and the Waynfleets live there too."

No emotion on the part of Twopence.

"And Archie says it's all to nothing that Cynthia and her sister

Pam will come down to their house while we are there."

"Will Miss Armstrong let us go?" said Twopence, who, though her heart pounded in uncomfortable exultation against her ribs, did not intend to rejoice until she was sure of her facts.

"I think so. Mrs. Falconer has written to Maynie—they knew one another when they were here at school."

"I wonder if Maynie knows the Waynfleets," reflected Twopence.

"Oh, you are glad, Twopence darling, aren't you? Do be glad out loud."

"You'd better change, or you'll get a bad mark for being late for tea," said Twopence, with a sudden access of virtue. "Yes. I'm glad."

She was glad, so glad that the feelings she had once associated with tempers alone—the feelings of little spikes at her finger-ends and behind her knees, began to prick and probe her—why, she did not know. Her excitement nearly made her lose Benjamin, so careless was she of his incarceration while she gave him some Madeira cake crumbs for his tea, and it caused her to forget her reserve with the Primroses sufficiently to sidle up to Archie and whisper, in the idiom she was learning to adopt, "I say, it's terribly good of you to have me to your place next week-end." And Archie had given her a nice friendly little grin which had made her wonder if Penelope were not right in having liked her so much from the very beginning.

Nor had her pleasure died down by next morning. Had she allowed herself to show it, it would have been less dangerous; hidden within her, and fighting to escape, it made her absent-minded, nervous, and awkward. At breakfast, as usual, she put the little receptacle for Peter's provisions on her knees, and, as usual, she glanced anxiously up the table to see what the meal was to be. Her face fell when a big tureen was placed before Miss Blencowe. Porridge! The most tiresome of foods to be transferred from a plate to a secret destination, and it made the box horribly messy. However, she had managed it before, and Peter liked it —probably it was very good for him, suffering as he did from a hacking cough.

She helped herself sparingly to milk, wisely considering that the more solid the porridge was the more easily it would be conveyed, and, eating slowly, with furtive glances at Miss Blencowe, waited her moment. Directly the mistress had begun breakfast she whipped two big spoonfuls from her plate, but her usual dexterity failed her, and, to her horror, she saw that she had deposited the mass on the edge of the box where it trembled for a second, and then, with dreadful determination, detached itself and slid, warm and spreading, on to her blue serge skirt.

"Theodora!"

Twopence jumped. The box fell with a sharp tap to the parquetry floor, and the mass spread further over her skirt. Her eyes gazed with horror at Miss Blencowe, who, nauseated, half rose from the table.

"Leave the room!" she commanded.

Twopence, clutching her skirt, managed to get up and stumble away. Lynette's big eyes became bigger; Archie, forgetting to control her spontaneous giggle, choked in her tea; Penelope sprang to her feet.

"Georgina, report yourself! Penelope, sit down!" And Miss Blencowe, with the expression of the bad sailor when the engines began to throb, sipped her tea, and nibbled a bit of dry toast.

Peter was waiting on the window-sill for his breakfast, and Twopence, thankful that he was there, suggested that he should lick her skirt, which he did with satisfactory thoroughness. As he was consuming the last delicious smears, the door opened and Miss Blencowe came in. At the sight of Peter she gave a little cry, for she detested cats, and he certainly was not a healthy specimen of his kind.

"Sh! Sh!" she hissed, flicking a handkerchief at Peter, who, accustomed to hostility, did not wait to vindicate his position, but immediately fled. "Don't you know," she went on, addressing Twopence, "that stray cats have horrible diseases? That cat is covered with mange—you will probably be infected."

Twopence said nothing. When she fought to keep down her anger she could not speak. Miss Blencowe looked at her. She prided herself on her excellent discipline, mingled with a complete understanding of each individual pupil. The submissiveness that Twopence had lately seemed to show had heartened her with a conviction of success with a difficult character. It had done this tiresome spoilt child good to be sent from the room on the first day, and her isolation in the Grey Dormitory had indeed been wisely decreed by the head-mistress. Now she was showing new vices—disgusting tastes and deceitful habits. Strictness had cured her temper; strictness would cure these things.

She looked round the room and saw the marks of muddy paws on the pillow.

"Do you mean to say that that cat has been sleeping on your bed?" she asked.

Twopence nodded. Her nails dug themselves into the palms of her hands, and she kept repeating to herself, "I promised Cynthia—I promised—I promised."

"Disgusting!" ejaculated Miss Blencowe. Then, with a quick gesture, she flung open the door of the cupboard in which Twopence, with the instinct of the good housewife, kept a reserve store for Peter and Benjamin, neatly placed by her paints, her books, and her Record of the Wee Poor Things. The mistress's horrified eyes fell on a piece of bread-and-butter, a chop bone, half a potato, a few toast crusts, and some haricot beans. Although these comestibles were carefully arranged on a piece of paper torn from an exercise book, they did not present an edifying spectacle, and there was some excuse for Miss Blencowe's gasp of dismay.

"This," she said, "is perfectly disgusting."

Twopence lost herself.

"You haven't any right to look in my cupboard!" she cried, her voice thick with anger. "It is mine, and I can keep what I like in it! And my food is mine, and, if I want to share it with Peter, I can! And I will! I will!"

She stopped, aghast. The red weight of rage had gone. Far away she heard Miss Blencowe's correct, accusing voice.

"There, my dear, you make a mistake. Privileges are only for those who may be trusted not to misuse them. That you will soon discover. At present you will remove that disgusting mass of food to the kitchen, before you attend your class."

Twopence stood motionless, not because she meant to disobey, but because, dazed by the tumult of anger and disappointment that raged in her, she could not quite realize what Miss Blencowe was saying to her.

"Do it at once!" repeated the mistress.

Twopence, with shaking hands, gathered up the paper, and folded its contents into an untidy parcel. Whereupon a subdued but passionate "Me-ow-ow" came from the window-sill, where Peter had once more ensconced himself, and, perhaps knowing that the fate of his meals had been decided, was watching proceedings with the concentration of despair. But his patroness did not hear him. Grasping the shameful parcel, her head bent, she crept after Miss Blencowe to the kitchen, aware that she had plunged herself in a sea of troubles, unable to guess, hardly caring, what the end might be.

She was soon to know. Reported to Miss Armstrong for further insubordination and insolence, she stood a poor chance. The head-mistress was a wise woman, but she was obliged to judge quickly, and she was accustomed to respect the opinions of her form and house-mistresses. She knew Miss Blencowe's limitations well enough, but she was better acquainted with the

more obvious ones of Theodora Wood. She was inclined to
believe that Theodora had "owned up" about that shield in a spirit
of bravado, though she had not been altogether unfavourably
impressed by her during that second interview. Miss Blencowe's
description of Peter made her smile a little, but the food hoard
would not do, and the assertion of rights that were wrongs was
just what Queen Æthelfleda's must subdue in a spoilt child. The
edict went forth—Twopence would not play games that Thursday
afternoon, and she would spend her half-term holiday in school.

CHAPTER IX

A HOLIDAY AT SCHOOL

"PLEASE, Mrs. Truefitt, may I go for a walk?"

Twopence, on the threshold of the matron's room, raised appealing blue eyes. It was a glorious afternoon, keen and sparkling with frost, and she had spent the morning darning stockings for herself and knitting mufflers for some unknown unit of His Majesty's forces. Mrs. Truefitt, who had expected her to be a nuisance, had been agreeably surprised at her docility, and, in answer to her questions, had furnished information as to her three sons, their full names, ages, heights, occupations before the war, and, as far as she knew, their present adventures on fields of battle east and west. It was impossible to be hostile to so interested a listener, and Mrs. Truefitt privately thought that Theodora Wood might have been forgiven and allowed to go to Morecott Marsh with Archie and Penelope. There was no denying that the cat was a nasty thieving brute, and that the child had no right to make a messy food hoard for him, but she had meant it kindly, and that was more than some people ever did, reflected matron, who was privately and publicly inconsolable for the demise of an obese and reserved feline, named Blot, and loathed, during his life, by Miss Blencowe. However, disgrace was disgrace, and she hesitated to allow a culprit a seldom-granted privilege.

"I don't know that I can come with you. I am expecting a few friends in to tea."

Half-term holiday was a mild festival for matron too.

"And you'll want some cake for them, and I'll get it," cried

Twopence, hands clasped. "I'll go so quickly and goodly. Och, let me go."

"If you go off on any of your pranks you'll get me into trouble," said matron doubtfully. The village was within school bounds, but she rightly suspected that Twopence wanted to go a little further.

"I'll tell you exactly where I am going," decided Twopence. "Just up there"—and she pointed to the spinney on the hill—"to feel the smell of the pines. And round by the lane where the wee crooked house is, and through the village home. It won't take an hour in all."

Somehow matron knew that it wouldn't, and that Twopence was not up to mischief. The spinney was only just out of school bounds, and it was a shame for the child to be in on an afternoon like this. She said she might go.

Twopence danced with elation as she pulled on the primrose cap she was still allowed to wear and wriggled into her coat. She almost laughed as she took the "Record of Wee Poor Things" out of her locker and tucked it under her arm. Her great desire since that fatal Thursday had been to conceal it—it would be dreadful if Miss Blencowe were again to search her cupboard and to find it and to read it. Enclosed in a tin vasculum she and Penelope had always used to carry provisions when they went picnicking, and concealed in the hollow of a tree she had climbed in the spinney— the abode of Penelope's Tree-You, as it happened—the precious volume would be safe, and she would find opportunities to add further records, which should be written in her own room and affixed to the pages of the Record. She had a pot of paste, which she slipped in her pocket, thinking it would be better to stow it in the hollow along with the vasculum than to leave it in that so-called private locker.

She ran all the way to the spinney, climbed the tree, and found a convenient hiding-place for her possessions in one of its forks.

This, on second thoughts, she preferred to the hollow, where they might have slipped down beyond her reach. She strapped the vasculum firmly to the branch, and concealed it with bunches of needles. When she stepped into the little lane where Penelope had met the Wounded Knight, she was quite out of breath, but glowed with satisfaction at the thought of having found a private place for her things.

Her contentment increased when she was joined by a couple of mongrels that she had often noticed in the village, and had christened Koosh and the Caramel dog. It was hard to say to what species Nature had intended these individuals to belong, but, as Koosh was shortish in the leg and shaggy, and the Caramel long, smooth and brown, they were as easily distinguishable from one another as if they had boasted pedigrees. They had been hunting in the spinney, but, having had no sport, decided to join Twopence, who walked as if she meant business. They had kind, honest eyes, and Twopence liked them. As she swung along she commanded them in a deep, fierce voice, "To heel, Koosh! Heel, sir!" "Heel, Caramel, you son of a mongrel!" and brandished a hazel switch she carried, as if to remind them of her power. The dogs occasionally obeyed her, just for the fun of the thing, and thoroughly enjoyed themselves.

"This," thought Twopence, as she approached the "wee crooked house," yellow, timbered, and, in spring, half-hidden by the blossom of its fruit trees, "this is where I should like all the Wee Poor Things to live."

Unconsciously she slackened her pace, thinking of Cynthia, who had been good to her, and the cripple whom she had been able to help, and whom she would have been glad to see again.

"Och, you darling!" she suddenly cried aloud.

From the gate came the tiniest, sprightliest dog that Twopence had ever seen—a Pekinese two-year-old, with a face like a black pansy, a shining red coat on which was one dark smudge, a plume of a tail, and a white forefoot. Twopence, having lived in a part of the country where toy dogs were infrequent, had not seen one of this breed before, and the impudence, daintiness, and spirit of the little grotesque that faced Koosh and the Caramel charmed her.

"Och, I would love to have it in my arms," she thought, as the mongrels, with doubtful waggings of tails, furtively sniffed the aristocrat. "Wee one ... darling ... come."

At this moment Koosh, deciding that this really would not do for a dog, sprang forward and stopped short with a low threatening growl, whereupon the Pekinese backed, and stood ruffling up her hairs, an angry little red dragon. Twopence reprovingly poked Koosh with her switch and gave an amused chuckle.

"Cinders! Lady Cinders! Come here at once! Call off your dogs, please! Call them off immediately!"

A very little lady dressed in stiff silk flounced down the garden path, as much out of temper as her small pet. Twopence, much abashed, ordered Koosh and the Caramel to heel, but the command was unnecessary, for Lady Cinders, with a shrill soprano bark, set upon them with such resolution that they fled incontinent. Lovable they might be, but they were mongrels, and as mongrels they showed themselves. Twopence blushed for them.

"Did you entice her out? Please catch her for me," said the little lady, trying, but not very hard, to conceal her annoyance.

Lady Cinders skipped a few yards from Twopence, and stood alert, ready for a game of skill.

"Oh, what *is* this?" Twopence exclaimed, kneeling on one knee and pretending to examine a find on the path. Immediately Lady Cinders, inquisitive as a monkey, bustled up, and in an instant Twopence had swooped upon her, and held her tightly and exultantly—she had caught one of the Tigh-na-Mara puppies like that once, and her stepfather had patted her on the back for her good sense. But the little lady did not compliment her. She said "Thank you," as if she hated having to say it, and, taking her Pekinese, strutted back to her crooked house, very dignified and thoroughly annoyed.

"Och, I should love to have known her wee dog, and I have offended her!" Twopence thought sadly, and, turning away, she walked quietly down the village, where she must call at the baker's for Mrs. Truefitt's cakes. Koosh and the Caramel rejoined her, but she did not speak to them. All the goodness had gone out of the day for her.

She was in bed—retiring for the night at seven o'clock was included in the stay-at-school punishment—when Penelope came back. As she heard her twin softly open the door she pulled the blankets over her head and pretended to be asleep, but Penelope knew this subterfuge, and was prepared for it.

"Twopence, darling, listen to me!" she said, sitting down on the bed. "Don't waste time—Blenks will be up soon, and it won't be healthy for me to be here then. Have you been very miserable? Mrs. Falconer said they might have let you come, and Pam Waynfleet said she wanted to see the kid Cynthia was interested in."

Twopence opened her eyes and emerged from the blankets before she had time to remember that, as far as Penelope knew, or as she thought Penelope knew, Cynthia's interest was nothing to her.

"The Falconers have a topping house!" went on Penelope. "Like the pictures of houses in father's book about Shakespeare's country—of course, this *is* Shakespeare's country. There's an old moat, and a secret stair, and four dogs, and a baby."

"Boy or girl?" inquired Twopence, thawing with unusual rapidity.

"Girl—oh, *sweet*, with darling wee finger-nails. And, Twopence! I've found out lots about Cynthia and her secret sorrow. So has

Archie—more than she ever knew. You see, Tony Dakeyne was there, and he was talking about Timmy Waynfleet, who is a soldier and missing, and probably killed. He was talking to Mrs. Falconer, and she said a lot about all the family before she remembered Archie and I were there, and asked us if we wouldn't like to go upstairs and see the baby in her bath."

"Go on!" said Twopence, sitting up and hugging her knees.

"Well, we went to tea with Cynthia on Sunday"—Twopence felt as if her heart had turned to stone and were hurting her—"and it was terribly nice, and her sister Pam is sweet, with jolly brave eyes, but she seems sad somehow, sadder than Cynthia. And their father didn't speak much, but you felt that he quite liked you being there. But, oh, Twopence, they're *fearfully* poor."

"How do you know?"

"Well, the house is wee, and as if everything rich had been taken out of it—but I liked it. And their mother is dead. And they are poor because of Timmy, the brother who was killed in France. He made friends who weren't good for him, and gambled, and got into debt. Then he was scared, and enlisted, and his father was fearfully angry about it, and paid up all the money he owed. And then the war came, and when he was missing his father was most dreadfully remorseful. All the spirit seemed to have gone out of him, Mrs. Falconer said, and she said she was sorry for Pam, and that the girl's life was a tragedy."

"And Cynthia?"

"And Cynthia too. Cynthia loved Timmy better than anything in the world. Pam loved him too, but Pam was engaged to someone called Uf-uf—did you ever hear such a funny name?"

Twopence remembered the three photographs in Cynthia's room.

"I remember something about him," she told her sister.

"Well, Pam, being engaged, hadn't so much to spare for Timmy. But Pam isn't engaged now, and Mrs. Falconer said it was a shame that your life should be blighted in your early twenties, and Pam gives music lessons to eke out the family fortunes—"

Penelope, pleased with the phrase, stopped to take breath.

"And Cynthia?"

"Mrs. Falconer doesn't think Cynthia will be able to stay at school till the end of the year, as things are. And it's a pity, because she wanted to work for a scholarship, and go to college, and earn her own living."

"Won't anyone give Cynthia the money?" said Twopence, her eyes wide and soft with pity.

"I don't know. Tony Dakeyne—he used to know Timmy, though he wasn't in the gambling set—said the family was exceedingly proud, and no one knew what—"

"S-s-sh!"

A footstep along the corridor. Penelope, never at a loss, darted under the bed and remained motionless. Miss Blencowe peeped in, glanced with satisfaction at the recumbent and deeply-breathing Twopence, and went on to the Primrose Dorm. Then Penelope emerged, with her triumphant smile.

"Good-night, dear; good-night, darling. Heaps of love from Penny," she whispered, taking her sister's hand into her own.

"Good-night, dear; good-night, darling. Heaps of love from Twopence," came the response.

It had been their formula as soon as they could speak sentences, and Twopence, though she had not known how much she had missed it since they had been separated, loved Penelope for remembering and saying it. How much better Penelope made her feel! And what interesting things she had told her! Left alone, she thought excitedly of the poor little house, of sad Pamela, of "Uf-uf," the wounded knight—"and I am sure he wouldn't blight anyone's life," she told herself loyally—of Timmy, who had been killed, of Cynthia. One fact she now knew—Cynthia wanted money. And how, how, could it be got for her?

CHAPTER X

The Twins at Home

WHEN grown-up people wish they were at school again they have forgotten many things. One of these is the sensation of helplessness which comes when you are, say, eleven, have threepence a week for yourself, and wish to make money.

Twopence rightly calculated that pennies, shillings, half-crowns would be of little use to Cynthia. She would need pounds. Queen Æthelfleda's was one of the best schools in England; Maynie had said so, and, though she did not find the life it offered particularly agreeable, Twopence, during the Christmas holidays, would have owned that Maynie was probably right. The place seemed better when viewed from a distance, and Cynthia, down at Morecott Marsh, became a goddess, enshrined, unapproachable.

On "hogmanay" Ian Muirhead, who sometimes forgot, remembered to bestow on the twins five shillings apiece. Maynie had presented them with strings of amber beads on Christmas Day. Penelope was delighted, but Twopence wished her stepmother had given her money instead. A casual visitor offered her half-a-crown to buy chocolates. There were no chocolates to be had in the vicinity of Tigh-na-Mara, and the satisfactory silver coin went into the little tartan silk bag which Kirstie had once bought for her as a souvenir of a holiday at Fort William.

All sorts of problems suggested themselves to her. How *could* she get enough to help Cynthia, even if she were able to save at the present rate, which seemed doubtful? If she amassed a big sum, how would she contrive to give it to a member of a family so poor and proud as Mrs. Falconer had said the Waynfleets were?

Would Cynthia be able to stay on for another term without her help? And, if she saved her threepence every week, how would she get food for Peter Leathery-Ear, Benjamin the Beetle, Koosh and the Caramel dog? Since the saving from her own meals had been discovered and forbidden, she had surreptitiously bought buns and bits of fish for them in the village. Twopence began to feel that the helping of the Wee Poor Things was a big responsibility.

The evening before they went back to school she had an idea, which she at once broached to her stepfather.

"Father," she said, "do you think, from my report, that my education is doing me any good?"

"Eh, what?" inquired Ian Muirhead, who was absently sketching Penelope on one of the white stone supports of the mantelpiece. He generally said, "Eh, what?" to a twin—never to Maynie.

Twopence repeated the question.

"Your report, Theodora Wood," said Ian, "is a document of great interest to a student of psychology, especially the psychology of the so-called, unjustly scorned, artistic temperament. It is, I suppose, also rather a pity."

Twopence seized what was useful to her in these remarks.

"I think so, too," she said. "Couldn't I stay here, father, and draw and paint in your studio, and couldn't you teach me to be an artist?"

"Not for worlds," said her stepfather, emphatically.

"And then I could have the money for my next term's schooling," pursued Twopence, who never left a thing half suggested. "I could find a splendid use for it."

"So could I," sighed Ian. "It's a great temptation to be a stepfather. Avaunt, thou fiends!"

Twopence gave herself a little shake of annoyance, and Maynie, who sat on a low stool by the fire, the pale green of her soft dress all shimmery in the light, looked at her and laughed. The twins were an eternal joke to their step-parents. Penelope had long ago given up trying to be taken seriously. Twopence could not give up things.

"What is it, Twopenny-bit?" said Maynie. "Do you want anything particularly badly?"

Twopence looked at her with deep and serious eyes.

"You're rather sweet, Twopenny. You'll be as pretty as Penelope some day, mark my words."

"Don't call her pretty," said Ian. "Even Penny doesn't deserve it, do you, Ariel?"

"*I* am considered beautiful," said Penelope, with a mincing, conscious look which she knew tickled her stepfather, and which she would produce for his benefit as a mother will make funny faces to amuse her baby. "Maynie, dear, were you at school with Pamela Waynfleet?"

"She was in the Third when I was in the Sixth," said Maynie quite sensibly.

"Oh, yes. And whom was she engaged to?"

"No one then, as far as I can remember."

Penelope gave a patient sigh, and Maynie repented.

"She was unlucky, Penny," she said. "I don't know much about it, but I do know that the man she was to have married wasn't much good—he led her young brother astray, or so people said—"

"That was Timmy! Timmy is dead now," said Penelope soberly.

"Yes. And the Waynfleets thought it was better for Pam to break off her engagement."

The heart of Twopence ached for one of her Wee Poor Things.

"There was some mistake," she said softly. "If it was the Wounded Knight she was to have married, he is good. I'm sure he is good."

No one seemed to hear her. Ian was whistling softly as he drew a blossomy bough by the side of Penelope's head. Maynie was staring into the fire, the fingers of her right hand playing with her big emerald ring; Penelope was thinking hard, her face unusually serious. And suddenly Twopence realized …

Penelope wanted to help the Waynfleets.

And Penelope would do it. She would hit on some splendid way; she would be first in the field, as she had been first to see and pounce on Cynthia's lost ball. It would all happen easily and beautifully—it would not be a half success, as so many successes are when you come to look at them closely.

Twopence thrust out her chin and shut her eyes, because hot tears were pushing up into them. The thing hadn't happened yet, but it was only a repetition of what had happened so many times before. Penelope was going in, and she, however hard she might try, was to stay out. That tremendous resolution, "I will give her out of kindness and my grateful sole whatever I can, but I know not what it may be," that silly wee tartan bag with its few shillings: these things would come to nothing. She could not think of a really good way to help; it must be because she was stupid and could not analyse a sentence, could not even remember what the dictionary and school thought the proper way to spell.

Suddenly something sprang up like a flame in her heart.

It was for Cynthia! If Penelope could think of a way, so much the better! It would help her, make her happy. What did it matter who did it? It would be better if everyone tried to help her—darling Cynthia Waynfleet, who had been frightened, and had conquered her fear, who had been sad, and hidden her sorrow, who had been hurt, and was too proud to exact apology. Twopence might be out of it—never mind! That wasn't the point—it didn't matter. If only Cynthia could be made safe and happy—

Twopence opened her eyes. An odd sensation passed over

her. "I feel," she said to herself, "as if tears were running through my soul." A strange thing was that, while ordinary tears make one feel sore all over, these gave Twopence a quiet kind of happiness, rather like that she had felt when Cynthia talked to her in the little bare room with the shadows of the flowers on the wall.

"You're very solemn, Twopence-ha'penny," remarked Maynie.

"She's thinking of ways to dispossess her cruel stepfather of the inheritance that should be hers," said Ian, who, next to Maynie, liked Twopence better than anyone he knew. "Are you wanting anything *really* badly, lassieky? I can gratify your desires, up to, say, four-and-six."

"No, father," said Twopence, shaking her head. "I don't think I want anything in the world just now. ... Though"—back-to-the-earth prudence made her add: "I should be glad of the four-and-six."

CHAPTER XI

SAVING FOR CYNTHIA

TWOPENCE resolved to speak to Penelope about Cynthia during the long journey south. It was odd that she should find it difficult to say anything to her twin, but they had passed Preston before she managed to tell of her great desire. As soon as she had done it she was glad—Penelope, though indirectly and unconsciously she could make a person feel a failure, had the gift of reassuring those who talked to her straight out about any subject important to themselves.

"I'm glad you have thought of it, Twopence," she said, "because I love the Waynfleets, and I'd love to help them. If we both try, we're sure to hit on something really good."

"It'll take ages to get the money," said Twopence, dolefully. She had decided to save a penny of her weekly allowance, which her stepfather had raised to sixpence, for Peter Leathery-Ear. Benjamin, whom she had taken up to Tigh-na-Mara, had considerably perished on the last night of the holidays, and his corpse, wrapped in shining transparent cracker-paper, and enclosed in a tin Oxo box, was being conveyed south for decent interment somewhere near Queen Æthelfleda's. Twopence loyally tried to be sorry he was dead, but his crumbs had meant a rather big bit out of Peter's bun. Koosh and the Caramel could forage for themselves, and the Wounded Knight and that Very Honourable Member, Cynthia Waynfleet, fortunately did not need food. Fivepence a week—it was very little.

"Save the pence, and the pounds will take care of themselves," said Penelope, with less than her usual tact. "Sorry, Twopence, darling. I know proverbs sound silly, but they are so comforting."

"I don't think so," said Twopence fiercely. "They make me feel as if I want to push someone or something—hard."

"Well," said Penelope, "I should go on saving, and you might get enough to help Cynthia to buy her books. She'll need lots of books for a scholarship exam."

Twopence was comforted.

"I think," went on Penelope soberly, "that what we must do is to find our Wounded Knight, if you think he's Uf-uf."

Twopence had told Penelope of the photograph in Cynthia's room.

"Why?"

"Because, you see, we might throw him and Pamela together. Then they would get married, and the money that what Pam eats costs would do to keep Cynthia at Queen Fleda's."

"Och, Penny," cried Twopence, lost in admiration. "And how do you throw people together?"

"That," said Penelope, "will need some thinking out. But, never fear, we'll find a way. The thing is—to discover the Wounded Knight."

"Do you think Pam eats all that?" said Twopence, doubts arising as she considered her twin's plan. "I thought Mrs. Falconer said Pam gave music lessons to eke out the family fortunes—so they'd really be poorer if she married Uf-uf."

"No, they wouldn't. You get terribly little for teaching music. I asked Maynie. She said it would keep an ordinary person in stamps and shoe-leather. Now, Pam's husband would pay for her stamps and shoe-leather."

"But Pam won't wear many shoes out now, if she's teaching all the time," argued Twopence. "And she won't use many stamps if she's not engaged to Uf-uf, for she won't be caring to write letters to anyone else. So she'll give her money to the family."

"Music teachers are very hard on their shoes," said Penelope patiently. "Haven't you heard Miss Jobberns beating time with her foot when Archie and Lynette play their duets? And Pam will write a good many letters, to ease her heart of its secret sorrow. Twopence, I *know*, deep down in myself, that it will be a relief if Pam marries Uf-uf."

"I think so, too," agreed Twopence, convinced at last. "I wish we knew his real name, and where he lives."

"If we did," said Penelope, "we might write two letters, one saying: 'Be at the spinney with the pines at 3 p.m. on January 18, and you will see something to your advantage,' and another saying the same thing, and post one to Pam and the other to Uf-uf, and so they would be thrown together."

"I think what made them annoyed with one another ought to be smoothed out first," said Twopence, cautiously. "I can imagine it making people simply furious to be thrown at one another while things still rankle."

"No," said Penelope. "If people really are in love they are willing to forgive directly they set eyes on one another."

Twopence felt that this was probably right —it was wonderful how Penelope always knew things.

"So, Twopence, what we have to do is to try to discover Uf-uf's real name and address, and to find out all we can about him and the Waynfleets, and tell one another—"

"And save for Cynthia," finished Twopence.

"That will be difficult," said Penelope.

And it was.

As well as sixpence a week for the gratification of their own desires, Penelope and Twopence had monthly half-crowns for odd necessary expenses, such as stamps and subscriptions. These half-crowns were always spent, and Twopence, calculating sources from which she might increase her hoard for Cynthia, had forgotten their existence. But when, on her return from the holidays, Matron handed her a bright florin and two threepenny bits with her weekly sixpence, her heart gave a jump of delight. Every contribution asked for in school was voluntary—some, such as that for the hospital bed, must be made, but some might be avoided, and avoided they should be, at whatever personal inconvenience.

During the first month all went well, and Twopence found her little tartan bag heavier by three shillings. Sixpence had gone to the bed; fourpence to Peter Leathery-Ear, eightpence to church collections. She had accepted Penelope's offer to enclose her weekly letter to Tigh-na-Mara in her envelope; she had resisted the craving for sweets which sometimes seized her. With satisfaction she made her entries in the Cynthia section of the Record of Wee Poor Things. She would not think of the probability that her hoard would never be a big one—the fact that it was increasing was enough for her. Like a small miser she handled and examined her coins every night—the crown-piece her stepfather had given her, on which she had scratched a "C," the half-crown, dated 1886, which the visitor had produced as a welcome substitute for chocolate, a few pennies, alike to the casual observer, but different, as Twopence knew, in thickness and shade, the shining milled shilling and the thin old one, the two sixpences, one with a hole, one a little bent. She loved to see the tall Cynthia moving proudly and lazily about the school, and to think that money that belonged to her was accumulating in a tartan silk bag, hidden far back in the locker of a certain Twopence Wood, insignificant but for this unknown link with greatness.

Then came February, when people think of flowers.

"We get a prize," explained Archie, "for the form-room that has the highest marks, and the form garden, and the dorm. The garden doesn't want any special attention just now—there are just the form and the dorm. The day girls help with the form, of course. We always get flowers the colour of the dorm. Daffodils are topping in this one. I saw daffodils in the shops to-day.

A penny a week from each of the form does for that—it has to be a little more for the dorm."

Twopence, who was sitting with Penelope on a bed in the Primrose Dorm listening to this, felt her heart sink. Fourpence a month gone for the form—but she would not be obliged to give to the dorm. Disgraced as she was, it would not be expected of her.

"You'll cobe id with us," said Lynette, who was suffering from what she called her "sprig affligshun," though, as Archie said, it was really unnecessary to distinguish seasons. Lynette had seen the anxious expression on the outcast's face, and had misinterpreted it.

Twopence thrust out her chin.

"I don't think I will," she said.

"Dodseds," said Lynette, still deluded. "You wear the Pribrose cap ad die—you are a Pribrose really, though you're id thad horrid little dorb."

Penelope, who loved Lynette for being nice to Twopence, put her arm round her twin's waist. For the moment she had forgotten the Cynthia hoard.

"I'm sorry," said Twopence, who also felt the kindness of Lynette. "I can't afford it."

Archie and Lynette looked puzzled, and Penelope remembered.

"Oh, well, that settles it," said Archie. "We must each give a little more, that's all."

"You needn't do that," said Twopence. "You can buy a few less flowers."

"And have fewer than the Roses and Violets? Great scheme, that."

"One person won't make much difference," said Twopence, desperately. "And you don't want many flowers—it's the colour that matters, and the kind of jar you put them in, and the way you arrange them."

"Thanks," said Archie, with dreadful sarcasm.

Twopence looked at her pleadingly. In the old days she would have flashed into anger at once; now she longed to justify herself. Archie and Lynette were Penny's friends, and she liked them too, and she could see why they disapproved of her. But she could not explain to them—it would not be fair to Cynthia.

"I'm sorry," she said, "but people haven't always money, you know. I'm short now—if I had it I'd buy tulips or violets or anything you liked for the Primrose Dorm. I will, too, some time—you'll see."

Archie and Lynette looked at one another. They, of course, knew what "weekly" and what "extra" money the twins had; they also knew that Twopence bought nothing for herself but a weekly bun—a bun that Archie had once seen her mashing up in her soap-dish with some milk conveyed from Mrs. Truefitt's room— Matron, who liked Twopence, had occasionally responded to the plea: "May I have a drink, please. I get terribly thirsty in the night," with something more nourishing than a glass of water. Archie had no idea of the existence of Peter Leathery-Ear, and she only hoped that Penelope's sister wasn't mad.

"It won't do us much good, as we shall have lost the prize then," she said. "Thank you, all the same."

The subject was dismissed—so, as she knew, was Twopence. She left the Primrose Dorm feeling desperately miserable. Had she done wrong? She ought to contribute towards those flowers, yet, if she once began to give for things like that, the money would soon be absorbed, and Cynthia's hoard would become less. It was hers, that half-crown, to do what she liked with, as long as she did not spend it directly on herself. The girls bought presents for their friends and relations from their monthly money—she was, in a way, buying a present for Cynthia—only Cynthia must never, never know. It was horribly difficult.

However, she meant to stick it out. The next day, acting on

the as-well-be-hanged-for-a-sheep principle, she did not give to the collection for form flowers. The captains would probably not have noticed the omission, for it was a tradition at Queen Æthelfleda's that no one should be asked directly for money, but Archie, who was really indignant with Twopence, pointed out that she intended to do nothing towards the reputation of the form.

"It is the end of the edge," she said. "One stands a lot because Penny is so decent, but I do think the time has come to protest."

"It's an insult to Blenks, when you come to think of it," said Margaret Marshall, the younger of the two form captains. Although Margaret was only twelve, she had the true ruler's instinct as to the uses of the sheltering phrase, and every defection on the part of the form she called an insult to Blenks—a description with which the individual in question would have heartily agreed.

"It's an insult to us, which is rather more important," decided the elder captain, who felt her position keenly. "And we must deal with it as such."

"She must have no end of money," said Archie. "She gets as much as her sister, and never spends a sou, except on revolting buns she mashes up with milk in her soap-dish and consumes in the dead of night."

"That settles it," said the elder captain.

So it came to pass that Twopence Wood, entering her little Grey Dorm that evening, found a large piece of exercise paper pinned on to her bed.

NOTICE.

TO THEODORA WOOD.

YOU ARE A MEAN MISER.

The "mean miser's" heart was in her throat. Turning over the paper with trembling fingers she read a list of signatures, headed by those of the captains, ended by Falconer, Georgina, and Mannering, Lynette M. Every Third Form girl had written her name there—in her best round hand—it was somehow additionally galling that they had all taken so much trouble— everyone except Penelope. Penelope probably did not know — and, if she did, she would have sense enough not to explain by telling of the hoard for Cynthia.

For a moment the walls rocked round Twopence, and she felt the tiny spikes at her finger-ends and behind her knees. Then, with a quick movement, she flung open her locker door. Out came her bottle of Indian ink and a camel's-hair brush. Below the signatures, in big letters, went the defiance:

I Don't Care.

Relieved, she undressed, bathed, and crept into bed, where, clutching a tartan silk bag, the strange and vivid conglomeration of whose colour was rapidly fading, she quickly fell asleep.

CHAPTER XII

THOUGH her defiance, laid next morning on the captains' double desk, afforded her some satisfaction, Twopence *did* care.

The Lower Third, having once got hold of the idea that Theodora Wood was a miser, did not easily relinquish it. Active persecution was stopped by Kate, who happened to come across a sample of it during half-time on the hockey-field, but suspicions, far from dying down, were heightened by many strange circumstances. Why did Twopence apparently prefer the solitude of the Grey to the sociable atmosphere of the Primrose Dorm? Why, unless to add to a private hoard, did she particularly like to go to the spinney, where, while the others played hide-and-seek for the benefit of Mademoiselle—the only mistress who could be convinced that this was more healthful than a crocodile walk— she would conceal herself so cleverly that no one ever found her? They did not guess that her longing to be alone came from the wretched consciousness of being different, of being a failure, or that the good hiding-place was in the branches of the pine-tree that kept the secret of her Record of Wee Poor Things—a book which, though sometimes slipped into the conveniently baggy blouse of youth and taken back to Queen Æthelfleda's for some especially important new entry, must always be restored to its own nook, where it would be safe from Blenks.

What good were her Wee Poor Things to her, Twopence began to wonder, and what good was she to them? Benjamin the Beetle was dead, and she hadn't had time to make him his promised "handsome toom." Peter Leathery-Ear had only a Saturday meal from her, and she daren't keep him in her dorm. and love him. The Caramel and Koosh, though they always welcomed her with uproarious demonstrations of affection, could have got on very well without her. She hadn't discovered the present address of the Wounded Knight, and she couldn't save enough for Cynthia to make it worth while to be called a miser. ... The people who managed to befriend waifs and outcasts, to do them real good, must be the Penelope people.

These were her thoughts one grey afternoon in late February, when little gusts and lifts of wind drove rain against the faces of the juniors who struggled back from their afternoon walk, shepherded by a mademoiselle whose feelings for once found no expression in words as she fought to control hat and umbrella and skirt, all of which had decided upon careering in different directions, and who was as wretched as the solemn little girl who trudged beside her, yellow cap pulled well down to her eyebrows, hands thrust deep in pockets. When they reached the door, and Primroses, Violets, and Roses, with sudden animation, rushed off to their dormitories, she leant helplessly against a pillar.

"Pouf! Mon Dieu!" she ejaculated. "Eet ees weecked."

"Matron wants you, Mamselle," said Twopence, with some sympathy, as Mrs. Truefitt's grey-clad figure, unobserved by the distressed Frenchwoman, appeared in the hall.

"Lynette Mannering is really rather worse this time," said Matron, holding out an envelope. "Could you take this prescription to be made up, Mademoiselle?"

"Mamselle's dead," said Twopence. "I'll take it—I'll run all the way, and wait for it, and bring it back."

Matron remembered with what alacrity Twopence had performed her mission on the afternoon of the half-term holiday. And the chemist's shop was not out of bounds.

"Hurry, then," she said, handing Twopence the prescription. "Straight there and back, mind."

Twopence was off, running as she always longed to do when she walked with a mistress and the other girls. Alone, with a message to do, she felt happy, and the weather seemed to improve. She liked the wild dash of a quick shower of rain, there and gone, the swift movement of the clouds, the little river, now in spate, rushing eagerly to cast itself over the weir, bearing withered leaves and broken twigs with it. "And they're dead!" thought Twopence. "They couldn't have a more exciting time if they were alive."

As she was about to enter the chemist's shop she heard a quick bark of recognition. There were Koosh and the Caramel, and there, prepared to embark upon a lifelong friendship with them, collarless, muddy, and with the uniquely rakish appearance of the debased aristocrat, was Lady Cinders.

Twopence gasped.

She had already made up her mind that, even with a pedigree longer than herself, Lady Cinders was a Wee Poor Thing. She must spend her life on a lawn or cushion or lead, when she preferred to roam the streets with common dogs. There was pathos, too, in her lack of suspicion of her own limitations—it was all very well for her to challenge red-jawed mastiffs to a stand-up fight, but the result might be a Lady Cinders limp, cold, and quiet for ever. And it was sad that any human being who met her would think it necessary either to steal her or to catch her and carry her back to where she came from. The little old owner of the crooked house had been rather cross, but Twopence thought she must risk unjust suspicion and see Lady Cinders home as soon as she had delivered the prescription.

She dashed in and out of the shop, only to see a red streak vanish round the corner at the end of the street. Koosh and the Caramel, not much interested in the aristocracy of China,

lingered by the door, waiting for their friend. But Twopence had
no time for them just now.

"She'll get interested in a rubbish-heap or something before
she has got far," she thought, as she ran at top speed down the
street. "Poor wee thing—she isn't used to looking after herself
on the road. Suppose she is run over by a motor! How dreadfully
that cross little lady would miss a wee darling like that!"

Round the corner she sped, narrowly missing collision with a
milk-boy, who turned to stare at her as she tore on, panting for
breath, but never slackening pace, trusting that her second wind
would come without being coaxed. How could a wee crooked-
legged thing like Lady Cinders run so quickly? She had thought
of a Pekinese spaniel as a lap-dog.

Cheers! On a strip of grass above the wooden bridge that
should span the river, but was now half covered, stood Lady
Cinders, barking with ferocious delight at a couple of moor-hens
that she had seen in the rushes. In terror, the birds pushed from
their hiding-place, and then, with creak of wings, flew heavily
across the water. The little dog, excited beyond measure by this
new and startled plaything, dashed after them, and, swept at once
from her foothold, began to swim. Pluckily she battled along,
but the force of the pale brown, sweeping water was too great
for her. At once Twopence saw that she was drifting down the
stream, towards the village, towards the bridge, below which
the withered leaves and branches were carried, with greater and
increasing speed, towards the crash of the weir. She did not stop
to think. A Wee Poor Thing was in danger, and her first impulse
was always the same—help. She flung herself into the stream,
and fought across by the wooden bridge, gasping with the bitter
cold of the water, which hit her chest as if with repeated blows.
She had swum in the loch on rough days—she was a splendid
swimmer, stronger than Penelope, though not so swift. But it
had not been as bad as this. These stupid quiet little English

rivers—who would have thought they had it in them? Clinging to a stanchion of the bridge, swayed backwards and forwards like a senseless thing by the rush of the stream, she reached out and caught the struggling little body of the dog, as it was washed towards her. Now back—she wouldn't try to swim again; she would clutch the bridge and make her way gradually along by it. Her fingers were so numbed that she could hardly grip the planks; her breath came in great groaning sobs. Lady Cinders, tucked under her left arm, shivered and shivered, but did not struggle, frightened for once into absolute obedience to a human being's wishes. She would be in her depth again in a minute, then she could wade. Och! the *mud!* With one tremendous effort she struggled out on to the bank, her heavy soaked clothes weighing her down, her legs covered with thick clammy ooze, her teeth chattering, her lips pale purple. A great languor seized her; she wanted to fall to the ground and lie still. No, she mustn't do that. She must walk and get warm. Faintly she began to drag herself in the direction of the crooked house. It seemed a long way to go. If only a cart would come along the road—but it was growing late; the afternoon milk had been delivered. She did not meet a soul. With her chin thrust out, her whole will exerted to make herself move, she staggered on. Lady Cinders licked her hand with a tiny cordate tongue, curiously warm. How could it be so warm when Lady Cinders was so cold? The wee thing! She was safe, anyhow.

Would the little lady be cross? It didn't matter much if she were—nothing mattered if she could just get to the crooked house.

It was there!

As if she were walking in her sleep, Twopence swayed and stumbled up to the door.

She put Lady Cinders down on the mat, and, in a stupid half-conscious way, laughed to see how tiny she was with her beautiful coat soaked and straight, and her plumy tail a hank of thread. She looked despairingly at the bell. Could she ring it, with her cold, cold fingers, that wouldn't bend as she wanted them to?

"Hull—o! What—"

The door was flung open, and a rush of pink and gold warmth came from it. There, looking down upon her, his eyes full of concern, was Pamela's Uf-uf—her Wounded Knight.

"It's the wee dog—"

The pink and gold somehow got behind Twopence's eyes and moved backwards and forwards like water, which ran down round her ears, and sounded near and yet far away. A long way off, the Wounded Knight was speaking—and how funny Lady Cinders looked, with her round head not a bit smaller, and her soaked body so wee …

Twopence doubled up. The Wounded Knight caught her before she fell, and, limping across the square hall very slowly, because, when it came to unexpected things like this, he couldn't say that his new leg was as good as his old one, laid her gently on a sofa, while Lady Cinders pranced up to the fire, shook herself, and looked round with plaintive eyes for suggestions as to what should be done to restore her to her usual health and beauty. From the back of the hall came the little lady in stiff silk—and she did not look cross at all.

"Elfric?" she said, and her voice meant, "Who is this little girl, and what is the matter with her?"

"Heaven knows," said the Wounded Knight, as if the question had been asked in full. "Hot bottles and blankets, don't you think?"

"Poor wee thing!" exclaimed the little lady, ringing the bell.

And though that small potentate, turning a swimming eye upon her, thought she did, she didn't mean Lady Cinders.

CHAPTER XIII

SUDDEN ILLNESS

She's a little light-headed, but she'll soon be perfectly fit," said the Wounded Knight, looking at Penelope. "But she's worrying about something—some Record of Wee Poor Things, she calls it."

Penelope, seated on the edge of a chair in Miss Armstrong's room, hands folded and eyes submissive, because she felt that such demeanour was only fair to a head-mistress, could hardly restrain her impatient desire to ask him question after question. Listening as hard as she could, she was struck, as she often had been, with the futility of the conversation between two sensible grown-up people not very well acquainted. She did not know the Wounded Knight any better than Miss Armstrong did, and yet she would have got so much interesting information out of him in half the time—things that really mattered about Twopence, and Lady Cinders, and, when these were told, perhaps, if she were clever and lucky, something important about Pam.

"Is it anything to do with a game you play?" inquired Miss Armstrong, lowering herself, with an effort of memory, to the level of eleven years old.

"No. It will be a private game of Twopence's—Theodora's, I mean. I'll try to find out about it."

"And shall I send a carriage for Theodora this afternoon?" suggested Miss Armstrong.

The Wounded Knight looked doubtful.

"Well, I think my aunt would like to keep her for a bit, if she may, thank you very much," he said stumblingly, and Penelope felt a little tickle at her heart, for she realized that he was a bit afraid of Miss Armstrong.

"I will write to Miss Thorne," said the head-mistress, in a reassuring voice. "It may be better that Theodora should not be moved. It is very kind of Miss Thorne. And her sister shall bring round the book she wants, if it is discovered. You may go now, Penelope."

Penelope went slowly up to the little dormitory. She would pack a suit-case for Twopence, and then, if holes had been sewn up instead of darned, Matron would not discover. And Twopence always forgot to thread ribbons through her nightgowns. Also the odds were that there would be something in the locker that should not be displayed to the eyes of an unsympathetic world—Penelope remembered Blenks and the food-hoard.

By substituting her own raiment for that of her sister, she made a quick and satisfactory job of the packing. She searched the locker, found the tartan bag, which she put at the top of the suit-case, but discovered no book likely to be that which Twopence wanted. Going over to the window, she stared thoughtfully out, remembering, wondering.

Her happy feeling came again as she looked at the spinney, growing dark against the cool gold of the afternoon sky. Then she was sure—

Twopence loved those trees. She had gone to them when she ran away; she climbed one of them and hid in its branches when the crocodile went to the spinney. Penelope knew, though she herself had always played with the others, the mysterious book she wanted would be there.

Penelope ran to the Primrose Dorm, pulled on her cap and coat and dashed down the drive.

She forgot that Miss Armstrong had said she must not go beyond school-bounds alone. In less than a quarter of an hour she was in the spinney, and she went at once to her favourite tree. Standing close to its trunk, she narrowed her eyes to see up among its branches—yes! she thought she could make out something small and square, strapped into a convenient fork. Wrinkling up her nose, for she hated the feel of bark on her hands, she began, slowly but easily, to ascend to the secret place. Once perched there, she wondered why she had not climbed the tree before—it was so dark and lonely and yet friendly, with the branches stretching around and above her, like walls and a roof—a house without a floor. She felt very close to the tree spirit now. But there was no time to enjoy the feeling—quickly she unfastened the vasculum, slung it across her shoulders, descended, and hurried from the other end of the spinney, down the lane, to the little crooked house. Drawing out the brown paper book, she handed it to the maid, who disappointingly came to the door, and, suddenly remembering that authority might condemn her for having taken the discovered treasure round to Twopence without immediate permission—her visit to the spinney need not be known—she walked rather soberly back to school.

"What an odd little kid she is!"

So the Wounded Knight, chuckling over Benjamin the Beetle and himself, as he turned the brown paper pages of the Record, while Miss Thorne, spectacles adjusted, leaned over his shoulder, anxious to ascertain what the extraordinary drawings and resolutions really meant.

"The child seems genuinely fond of animals," she said approvingly, glancing from the entry about "Peter Lethery-Ear" to the cushion where Lady Cinders, none the worse for her adventure, reclined in luxury, her black pansy face turned towards the readers as if she, too, were interested in the benefactress of Wee Poor Things.

"And people. I rather think, from his 'sine,' that I must be a 'Woonded Nite.'"

"'Cynthia Waynfleet'? Are those the Waynfleets you used to know, Elfric?" she asked him.

"Couldn't say. There *was* a Cynthia, of course."

The Wounded Knight was solemn all of a sudden. There was a Timmy, an unhappy Timmy, whose bad luck had a way of extending itself to his friends, and there was, and always would be, as long as he and she lived, and perhaps longer, a *Pamela*.

"Here she is again."

He turned over the pages telling of the "Karamell Dog" and "Koosh"—"who are iggnorant of their teribbel lak of curtesie, and must be taut to know better," to a page of figures.

AKOWNT OF MY HORDE
for Cynthia Waynfleet
who is likely to endure hardship for lakk of looker—

	£	s.	d.
From Mr. McAndrew, a wellcom visitor			
for chokkolat		2	6
From my good steppfather on Hogg Manay		5	0
Church collekshuns (the caws not being speshial)			6
Saved from eggstra monney		1	0
” ”		1	0
Pokket money			6
” ”			6

N.B.—This does not appere a grate sum, but who knows? Cynthia Waynfleet, a Very Honourable Member, may have some relashun who will innvest it for a large profit.

"That she hasn't!" cried the Wounded Knight, laughing again. "This is a business lady, isn't she? 'A large profit!' When she learns to spell, there'll be no gainsaying her schemes. But won't it be a loss?"

"She is a kind little girl," said Miss Thorne. "It is a pity she has not been taught to spell. Poor child, she seems very backward."

"Priceless!" murmured the Knight, turning back to the description of Benjamin's benefits.

"Are these Waynfleets so poor?" inquired Miss Thorne, rather nervously. What her nephew's relationship with Pamela had been she was not quite sure, and her own delicacy of feeling, and knowledge of his proud sensitiveness, made her afraid to question him.

"I believe so, now. They used to be quite well off." He evidently did not want to discuss them, and, with a repressed sigh, the little lady took the book and carried it up to the room where Twopence lay. For a few moments she stood by the bed watching the child, who, though she tossed and moaned, slept—slept after a night and day of difficult breathing and feverish talk of Peter starving, of Lady Cinders being so funny when she was wet, of the cold water, of money in a tartan bag, of hockey and being lonely, of Penny finding a good way. And most of all, of a Record of Wee Poor Things, which someone might find, which she wanted under her pillow. Miss Thorne put the book beside her, that she might find it there when she awoke. She stood a little longer, thinking. She was angry with herself for having spoken so sharply to this Theodora Wood when she had caught Lady Cinders so cleverly some weeks ago. The milk-boy had told her maid how he had seen her run after the little dog yesterday—the sequel to the chase she could only guess at, but she guessed fairly accurately. Sharp-tongued as she was, she too loved to help—her motherless nephew had come at once to her when he was discharged as unfit for service, and, though he was restless, and eager to get away and work at what he could still do, she felt that he would always come back. The prospect of nursing a sick child was positively pleasurable to her. But she only loved the well-favoured and the well-bred—her pets had always been pedigree. Something quite different was touched in her heart by Twopence's protection of a stray cat, "thin and

Most Dejekted in his ribs," of a beetle, "foe tho innocent of all wommen," of a couple of ugly unloved mongrels, something which gave her that strange new feeling which may come when you are quite old, the feeling that Twopence had thought was like tears running through her soul.

"Poor little girl," she thought. "I should like to help her. Beetles perhaps are beyond my scope, but we must see if anything can be done for this Cynthia Waynfleet."

CHAPTER XIV

GOOD NEWS

WHEN she had once made a resolution, Miss Thorne never waited to put it into practice longer than she could help.

Twopence was a quick recoverer. In a few days the fever that came from cold and exposure had gone, and, impatient of bed, but happy because the cross little lady had turned out to be so kind, she was sitting propped up by pillows, ready for any number of visitors. But at first Miss Thorne, beyond five minutes of Penelope, would not let her see anything of anyone. "One cannot be too careful, dear," she said. Twopence considered this an appalling standard of conduct, but did not find it difficult to submit, under the circumstances. They were quite pleasant and interesting. Lady Cinders was one of them, and Twopence saw her pedigree, and heard how all the Ashleigh Morrell family had that black smudge, which marred, as some thought, the redness of their coats. Then there were the box of quaintly shaped old jewels, the solitaire board with the clear glass marbles with their fascinating insides, the albums in which the friends of Miss Thorne's mother had executed fine drawings of roses and shells, and penned noble though rather obvious sentiments in tiny copperplate, the crazy quilt which the old lady had made in her youth, every patch of which told the story of a pretty frock, or a fine flowered petticoat, and the stamp snake, with the flat green velvet head and the red flannel tongue. Miss Blencowe would not have recognized her tiresome pupil in the convalescent who sat wrapped in the Paisley shawl, the patchwork quilt drawn well up to her chest, Lady Cinders and the stamp snake (who felt prickly, dusty, and heavy, but waggled most ingratiatingly) beside her, her eyes sparkling, with interest as she listened to her hostess's reminiscences, her voice tender and eager as she told of Penelope and home. In an astonishingly short time the two knew one another, as a child and an old woman often will do. Then Miss Thorne saw her opportunity, and spoke.

"You must not think it impertinent of me, love," she said, "but I must confess to having overlooked your Record of Wee Poor Things, as you call it, and I should like to speak to you about them."

Twopence turned very red. There was probably something silly in her plans—Maynie and her stepfather were always much amused if they happened to discover any of her or Penelope's secret schemes, and she hated being laughed at.

"That poor cat, for instance," said Miss Thorne, going bravely on. "Perhaps he might come here to stay until you are better. Jessie could call on one of the servants at Queen Æthelfleda's, if you think it might be possible to procure him."

"Rather!" cried Twopence, with shining eyes. "All Jessie need do is to stand by the gate with a bit of fish or something with a strongish smell and say 'Puss, puss,' Peter would come from wherever he was."

"That is excellent," said Miss Thorne. "Beetles, my dear, I was never very partial to, but, in any case, your pet is dead. For the dogs we might find homes. I will have them here for a short time first."

"Och, you *are* good!" Twopence was touched to the heart. "I might wash them in the garden, if you would let me, and brush them and smarten them up a little—they'd be quite bonny dogs then. And a little love and training would improve them so much."

"So I think, love. And what is this about Cynthia Waynfleet?" Twopence flushed again.

"I don't know if I should talk about her," she said cautiously. "Penny heard quite accidentally that she might have to leave school, she's so poor. And the family is very, very proud."

"Is she a clever girl?"

"Ever so clever. And she is good and kind."

Tears came to Twopence's eyes. She was always disappointed that she had been unable to do more for Cynthia.

"Well, I have been thinking out a plan," said Miss Thorne. "I have a little money that for some time I have wished to give to some educational institution. If a scholarship, available for a girl's last year at school, and paying all expenses, were offered, do you think it probable that your friend would obtain it?"

"Your friend!" Twopence clasped her hands round her knees in a kind of ecstasy. Cynthia her friend!

"She's much the cleverest girl in school! She's head girl!"

"A scholarship for the head girl, then, dating from the first of this year."

"This year!" Twopence bounced up and down on the springy bed. "Och, I do love people who do things straight off. It makes them seem a hundred times more. When is Penny coming to see me, Miss Thorne?"

"As soon as you like, love. This afternoon, shall we say?" Miss Thorne, pink with exultation at the success of her scheme, was in no mood to deny visitors to Twopence.

But Penelope did not come till later; it was the Wounded Knight who was the first to hear of the generosity of Miss Thorne. He limped up the stairs and played a little tune on the door with his silver pencil-case—a splendid substitute for knocking, thought Twopence. She gave a wriggle of pleasure as he came in, his eyebrows drawn together for the quizzical look he had for small girls, though his eyes were always so interested and kind that they knew he wasn't laughing at them.

He sat down on the bed and produced an oblong piece of

wood, nicely rounded at the top and he had managed to paint it to look exactly like black marble.

On the "headstone" in gilt letters, was the inscription:

COURTEOUS MEMORY OF

BENJAMIN,

AN ORNAMENT TO HIS RACE, THOUGH THE

INNOCENT FOE OF WOMEN.

HE DID WHAT HE COULD.

And, at the back, in very small lettering:

"Erected by the Wounded Knight."

The Knight looked hopefully at Twopence as she examined his work. She would never know what a struggle he had had to forego the delight of reproducing her spelling, a sacrifice he felt to be necessary, in case she should think he laughed at her.

"I thought you probably wouldn't have time to put up the tomb you promised," he said. "If you think it's cheek for me to butt in with this—"

"It's a beautiful tomb," said Twopence, shyly.

The Wounded Knight breathed again.

"Did you read my book?" demanded Twopence.

"Well, yes. I'm afraid I did. I'm awfully sorry if it was private. It was so interesting. I simply couldn't stop when once I had begun."

Twopence gave him a keen look. No, he wasn't laughing at her.

"And you'll admit I have a sort of right to read about the society I belong to," he went on seriously.

Twopence gasped.

"Och, you mustn't think it awful of me to call you a Wee Poor Thing," she whispered. "I don't really mean to mix you and Cynthia up with beetles and cats and mongrels. It was only that I was so sorry about—about—"

"I hope you like Cynthia and me better than Benjamin, really."

"Och, there's no comparing you," cried Twopence anxiously. "I never was fond of him—no, I don't mean that. I had a sort of feeling for him, but one can't care very much for a person like Benjamin. But," she added honestly, "I am very fond of Peter Leathery Ear."

"I hope to meet him soon."

"Yes. Things are happening so beautifully. Miss Thorne is giving a schol, which Cynthia will get, as she is head girl, and all the strays are to have happy homes. So there'll be no Wee Poor Things left."

The Wounded Knight looked at her queerly.

"Oh, yes, there will," he said. "There'll always be hundreds of 'em. So you mustn't bust up your society."

"I think I must," said Twopence. She couldn't explain to him that it would be impossible for her to continue it when people knew about it—he would think she was offended because her record had been examined, and it wasn't that. If Miss Thorne had not looked at it, Cynthia would not have been helped.

"It's a pity for all of us," said the Knight.

Twopence looked at him. He must still be unhappy about Pamela. Nothing had been done for him and Pamela. How glad she was that she had not recorded Penelope's idea of helping Cynthia through them! If he knew about it she would feel shy with him, the poor sad Wounded Knight! He must be kept from brooding, anyway.

"Let's have a game of bezique," she proposed, knowing that there is nothing like double bezique or sequence to make a man of you, and trusting that one of these plums might fall to the Knight. But he had not a chance to prove his luck, for no sooner were the cards shuffled and dealt than Penelope appeared, and, after greeting her as if she were an old friend—as he felt she was, because he had done her a service—he left the two together.

"What about your letter scheme, Penny?" said Twopence,

when the scholarship had been discussed and applauded. "Cynthia is all right now, but Pamela and Uf-uf aren't."

"Well," said Penelope, "I have been thinking it over, and I think letters are risky. People are easily put off by letters— they think someone is pulling their leg—I mean legs, or they're frightened. Or they might find out, and think we were interfering. No, I have a better scheme than that."

"What?"

"I'm going to stay with the Falconers again, the week-end after this. I'll wangle Pamela over to a certain place, and you'll wangle the Knight there at the same time. It's quite accidental, and, if she gives a cold bow and passes on, there's no harm done. But, if he says '*Pamela!*' and she says 'Oh, *Elfric!*' then *we* pass on—I'm afraid we shall *have* to—"

"For their sakes!" said Twopence, heroically. "But how *do* you wangle people to a certain place?"

"Uf-uf will be easy for you," said Penelope. "Pamela will be more difficult, because I don't know her very well, but I will find a way. Getting asked to the Falconers again was the most complicated thing, and that has wagged. Archie is simply set on taking me home with her for the half-term holiday now, and I don't think she had thought of it a few weeks ago. Cynthia isn't going home—she wants to get on with her work. You take the Knight up to the spinney between three and three-thirty on that Monday afternoon, and, if it doesn't come off, then it doesn't."

"But it will!" cried Twopence.

And Penelope thought it would.

CHAPTER XV

The Wounded Knight and Pamela

"As it is my last Monday," said Twopence, "I should like to choose what we shall do."

"Any old thing," said the Wounded Knight gallantly. "We'll go over to Birmingham for a picture-house and tea. Or—though I should much rather not—we'll take the Caramel and Koosh for a walk."

"They can't help it," said Twopence quickly. "And they look so much better now they are clean."

"Personally, I think that the earth helped to cover up deficiencies. So it's to be that. Righto. Only give me time to put on my disguise."

"You don't mean it!" said Twopence, with her deep and serious look. "I saw you indulging Caramel this morning—throwing stones for him, though you were terribly sick of doing it."

"*For* him? *At* him, you mean!"

"We won't argue the point. I don't want to go for a walk with him, anyway. I want to go up to the spinney."

"Where the gallant lady helped the Wounded Knight. Romance, romance! And we'll carve the whole story on a tree."

"We will not," said Twopence, with a look that was intended both to crumple up the Knight and to show him what good friends they were. "We will bury Benjamin, and you will erect the tomb you made to mark his grave."

"A funeral for the last festivity! O Scotland, Scotland!"

"I'm not altogether Scotch," said Twopence, giving him a little push. "And it won't really be sad, and I must get that Oxo box with Benjamin's remains out of the way. I can't bury him when I get back to school—you can't do anything there but learn lessons and play with balls."

"M-m-m-m. I must give Miss Armstrong a hint before she issues her new prospectus. Healthy situation. Gravel soil. Games and funerals a speciality. Large playing-fields and cemeteries."

Twopence left him.

"If only Penny has wangled Pamela," she thought, as she searched for her primrose cap, which was lost as often and as easily as a boy's. "But she will have. Penny can wangle anybody."

All the same, her confidence was dashed as they walked up the hill. There was not a soul to be seen, and, when they stepped into the spinney it was so quiet that, as the Knight said, they could almost hear the buds cracking open into little leaves. A few early anemones sprang from among the dead brown rubbish of last year, light and scentless and frail, as if the hard earth refused to give them colour and strength and fragrance. "They're like wee ghosts of things that have never died," said Twopence, and bit her lip, wondering if that were sense now that it was spoken. But the Wounded Knight said: "That's right, I think." He had become silent, as if he, too, were waiting for something to happen. The Oxo box was deposited in a mossy grave; the headstone erected; the grave trimmed with ivy. Twopence went through the ceremony without paying much attention to it. She constantly glanced about, longing to see the yellow cap, to hear Penelope's gay triumphant laugh—she would be sure to laugh if she had wangled Pamela. But there was no sound, except from a thrush who had flown into the spinney and was practising his spring song—a few notes over and over again.

Twopence felt desolate. It was sad that she could not ask the Knight about what was on her mind—he could laugh and tease her, but he would never, never speak to her about his troubles. It was strange, too, when she would have been so very sympathetic, but perhaps sympathy was of no real use, perhaps it did good just a little way down, as Peter Leathery Ear's rubbings and purrings did. Ah, but there was the Cynthia Waynfleet kind—

Scrunch! Scrunch!

A steady tramp of human shoes through the dead dried leaves, a clear voice singing a bit of a song.

> "Since first I saw your face I resolved
> To honour and re-*nown* you—"

Only one person! Bother! And she would stay here in the spinney rummaging among the bushes for primroses, spoiling everything when Penny *did* bring Pamela along.

> "If now I be—ah—ah—ah—ah—
> My heart had never known you."

Like most people who sing out of doors, she didn't know the words properly.

The Knight, who had been gazing abstractedly at Benjamin's grave, turned and stared in the direction from which the voice came. His eyes were different from the half sad, half quizzical ones Twopence knew. She had never seen a person's eyes look like that—

Her heart began to thump.

> "What! I that um-m-m-m-m
> Shall we begin to *wrang—le—*"

The song broke as the singer jumped the ditch bounding the spinney on the south, pushed through the bushes, and came into sight.

Hat under her arm, rough tweed coat, a streak of hair across her forehead, head erect. ... Cynthia, but with so much more certainty of herself—energy, fearlessness, resolution.

And all at once her eyes changed with the same strange look that astonished Twopence in the Knight's.

"Pam! My dear—my *dear!*"

Yes! Yes! Penelope had wangled it! Twopence, suddenly conscious of herself, though the others had suddenly forgotten her existence, honourably turned and fled.

CHAPTER XVI

Behind the Scenes

Y ES. It worked, but it really wasn't a *terribly* good way."

"Och, Penny!"

"It wasn't. There was a 'scusable lie in it, and if you can wangle a thing without a 'scusable lie, it's far better to do it."

"And what did you say?"

"You're panting. Let's sit down on this stile and rest."

It was true that Twopence was breathing hard and short—excitement, increased by the appearance of Penelope, half-way down the hill, had temporarily winded her. She submitted to being pulled down on the wooden step of the stile leading to a field-path, and, with eager eyes, leant forward to listen to her sister's story.

"I made Archie take me to call on the Waynfleets, because I had a secret message from Cynthia for Pamela. So I saw Pamela alone, and she kissed me, and asked how I was, and how I made my hair curl so nicely. And I said splendid, thank you, it's nature, and she said oh you're a lucky infant, and I said that's not what I've come about it's Cynthia and she rejoined well go ahead—" Penelope, whose narrative had got up a tremendous speed, gave a great gasping gulp, and paused.

"Well, do," said Twopence, sympathetically.

"I am," said Penelope, drawing a deep breath. "I said she wants to see you about something very private up in the Hill Spinney between three and three-thirty on Monday afternoon, and she said oh she never mentioned it in her letter, and I said funny but perhaps it's too private, and she screwed up her nose to think, and said yes perhaps it is—"

"Go on!"

"And she came by our train—"

"S-s-sh!" Twopence clutched her twin's arm. "There she is—no! it's Cynthia—coming along the lane with a soldier."

"Quick!" Penelope was over the stile and crouched behind a clump of just flowering gorse before the voices had become properly audible. Twopence followed her, with difficulty restraining a howl as a prickle fixed itself in her leg. Taking off their yellow caps, they huddled side by side, entirely concealed from the road and the stile.

"It's simply rotten!" the deep voice said.

"Timmy, it isn't!" Penelope and Twopence clasped hands at the sound of that usually lazy voice, now thrilled and broken and quick with excitement. "Nothing is rotten now you've come back. Oh, Timmy!"

"Except me."

"Don't!"

"Sit down, Cynthie. We must talk this over."

The two sat down on the stile, Cynthia settling her feet on the step.

"*Why* didn't you come home before?"

"Couldn't."

"Oh, Timmy, I was *dying* to know about you. I have never been happy since you went away."

"I know. I haven't either. But I knew you wouldn't *die*; you wouldn't let a chap down like that. And I always meant to let you know first, when I did come home—when I felt sure I should be welcomed."

"Timmy, you *are* an ass!"

"Not such an ass as you think, my dear. You didn't hear that interview between me and our paternal relative, please to remember."

"You might have known he wouldn't keep that up! But I'll hear the next, when you show him your ribbon."

"Don't. That's what makes me sick. And there's Uf undecorated just because people didn't know—didn't see. I say it again—if he hadn't crawled out to try and drag me back he wouldn't have lost his leg. ... I knew. ... I knew everything that was going on, only too horribly well. And now you tell me our rotten family has given him the push—"

"They didn't know, Timmy—we didn't know. Father said he had ruined you."

"Stuff! As if a chap like Uf could ever ruin anyone. Besides, it's such a jolly insult to me. I may have been a triple-extract ass, but, anyway, I was an ass on my own responsibility."

"I know, Timmy, I know," Cynthia calmed him. "I'm sure you were."

Too agitated, as was his sister, to notice the implication, Timmy continued.

"Pam *ought* to have known. Hang it all, she was *in love* with Uf."

"But Father and Uf had a tremendous row after you had gone, and then Father and Pam had another, and Uf and Pam seemed to work off the results of the two rows on one another—oh, Timmy, it was an awful time! You know what tempers Uf and Pam and Father all have! Then Uf disappeared. We guessed, of course, he was fighting, and Pam was always searching the papers for news of him, though she never said a word about him. And one day she found him in the 'Dangerously Wounded' list. It nearly killed her!"

"Umph!" grunted Timmy.

"It's true! She wrote to the only relative of his she knew, his uncle, you know—but her letter was returned. The uncle had gone to America, in the early days of the war. She got his address, and wrote again—and I believe she thought of writing to Uf, but, if she did, I don't think she posted it. Anyway, she heard nothing—"

"Well, Cynthie," said Timmy, impressively, "we all owe it to Uf to crawl about before him and let him wipe his feet on us."

Penelope began to giggle, but Twopence gave her a warning pinch.

"Oh, Timmy, supposing he doesn't care for Pam now!"

"If he has a particle of inclination for her, she shall be his, or my name isn't Timothy Waynfleet."

"What!—Why!—TIMMY!"

A flying rush, and Timmy rocked on the stile, as Pamela, who had come round the bend of the lane with the Wounded Knight, flung her arms round him and hugged him as if she never meant to let him go.

"Uf!"—"Timmy, what luck!"—"Cynthie? My only aunt, *hasn't* she grown up? So *this* was your private message, Cynthie?"— "No?" "Cheerio, old lad, give you my blessing." "Timmy!" "Uf!" "Cynthie!" "Pam!" "Oh, Timmy, *darling!*"

Penelope and Twopence, hugging one another, made no effort to restrain delighted gurgles of laughter. No one was likely to notice or to hear them now. They had done their bit; the scapegrace Timmy and Fate had done theirs.

"I wonder if we *ought* to have listened," whispered Penelope, as the party by the stile moved off. "But we couldn't have got away without being seen."

"The Knight has forgotten all about me," said Twopence, sadly emerging from her hiding place.

"You must excuse him, Twopence, darling. You see, it's a Supreme Moment in his life."

"*We* needn't have bothered to throw Pam and Uf-uf together, I suppose," went on Twopence, disposed to be pessimistic in the reaction following the tremendous excitement of the last quarter of an hour. "Timmy would have done it."

"Yes, but it wouldn't have been the same. Don't you see, they know they're in love now, in spite of the misunderstanding about Timmy and the tempers and father and *everything*. That's heaps more important than if Timmy had said, 'Uf is a hero, and my sister shall crawl about at his feet, and shall be his.'"

Twopence laughed. Penelope had got Timmy's intonation perfectly.

"You are right, Penny," she said admiringly. "You are always right, of course."

"So are you. Think of that schol for Cynthia. Hurrah! Three cheers for *US!*"

"Hip, hip, *hurrah!*"

Up went the primrose caps in the air, and then the twins pulled them on and walked quite calmly back, Twopence to the crooked house, Penelope to Queen Æthelfleda's, busy thinking their exciting thoughts.

CHAPTER XVII

A Farewell Party

EXCEPT the first by firelight, there are no teas jollier than the first by sunlight. So Twopence thought, as, sitting at the head of the table in Miss Thorne's pale yellow parlour, she looked proudly down at her party—the party that the little lady had insisted she should give on the last Saturday before she returned to school.

Over the big bowl of jonquils ("Not daffodils, love. There is a difference") she could see Miss Thorne, very busy over her wonderful old Queen Anne silver and Chelsea china, ascertaining exactly how much sugar and cream everyone liked or didn't like, and forgetting as soon as she grasped handle of spoon or jug. "It is because you confuse me so, love," she told the Wounded Knight, who, next to her, was trying to organize things by putting sugars to her right and non-sugars to her left. "I don't follow your military methods." Whereupon Timmy said he didn't wonder, and Pamela took the Knight's hand to comfort him.

There was an empty chair to the left of Twopence, waiting for Penelope, who had spent the afternoon playing in a Third Eleven practice, and on her right sat Cynthia, who was not too much preoccupied with the joy of the newly-found Timmy to talk to her a great deal. Peter Leathery Ear, growing sleek and glossy with good feeding and constant brushing, occupied the arm of the chair, the nearest possible place to his patroness, and, in anticipation of benefits to come, alternately lifted and planted his paws on his perch, to the accompaniment of loud raucous purring. Lady Cinders, confident that, whatever she did, everyone would love her, danced from place to place, exacting caresses until there should be a chance of cake. And the Caramel and Koosh, half exasperated and half amused at the large blue bows with which Twopence had decorated them, did not in the least object to the epithets which the Knight from time to time bestowed upon them, a certain tone of voice accompanied with threatening physical gestures being the only abuse they recognized.

"Why are Lady Cinders and Peter wearing orange and the others blue?" asked Cynthia. "Is it to distinguish the classes from the masses? It can't be, because Peter—"

"S-s-sh!" warned Twopence, adding in a low voice, "I like orange for them best, but there wasn't quite enough, and I didn't want the Caramel and Koosh to think they were wearing the others' left-over bits."

A knock came at the door.

"It's Penny!" cried Twopence. "Come in!"

And, as Penelope entered, cheeks a deeper pink than usual and eyes shining with physical exertion and lust of victory, Twopence suddenly realized that, for the first time in their lives, she had asked Penelope to come in. This was her party. No, it wasn't. She wanted it to belong to Penny too. Pamela was Penny's, and so was Timmy, who was saying: "Hullo, Penthesilea! How many have you laid out?" But, oh! it was good to feel that she wasn't out of it, that she had got in, how or why she didn't know—unless— unless—could it be through her Wee Poor Things?

She looked gravely round at them all—the Wounded Knight with his face screwed up with laughter at some foolish remark of Pam's, Peter Leathery-Ear purring satisfaction, the Caramel and Koosh warm and jolly and, considering the disadvantages of their upbringing, polite in their behaviour. Last of all she gave a shy glance at Cynthia, who seemed as if she were surrounded by a quiet light of happiness. Cynthia saw the glance, and smiled.

"Isn't it a lovely party, Twopence?" she said. "I don't think I have ever been so happy in my life."

"I know I haven't," said Twopence, looking at her toasted scone, and wondering if joy always took away one's appetite.

"Oh, Twopence," said Penelope. "I mustn't forget. Archie and Lyn send you their love, and Lyn says she owes you special thanks for ordering her cough mixture, which was the nice kind."

"If I hadn't gone, heaps wouldn't have happened," said Twopence, reflectively. "Tell Lyn I hope she is better, but that I owe *her* a lot for her 'affligshun,' will you?"

"I owe Lyn a lot too," said Cynthia, in a low voice. "Lyn, and someone else."

Twopence glowed. The Wounded Knight perhaps had not needed the help of her "strong rite arm," Peter and company could not tell her how they felt, but Cynthia Waynfleet, that Very Honourable Member, whom she had despaired of benefiting, could, and did, say that she was glad.

More than that, Twopence *felt* she was glad, felt the friendliness that would not be spoken, because Cynthia was not the kind of person to spoil things by saying too much. Uf-uf had had time to tell his new sister-to-be of the Record of Wee Poor Things, and of the pathetic hopefulness of that "akownt of my horde," and because Cynthia's pride was real, and not a thing assumed to give herself false dignity, it was not offended by this strictly private and passionate desire to help. She laughed, as Uf-uf did, but, remembering rumours of the persecution of a "Mean Miser," she realized that, in this little violent-tempered girl, lived the pity, the sacrifice, the loyalty of real friendship.

A silence had come over the party—a silence that did not matter because everyone was thinking of some special thing.

Miss Thorne thought—"This Cynthia seems a promising girl. 'Isabella Thorne scholarship: Cynthia Waynfleet,' will look well on the list of school honours, very well. I am glad the idea was suggested to me."

And Timmy—"Wonder why I felt it a risk to come home— jolly infants, those twins."

And Pamela—"What a splendid profile Uf has! How decent of that little Penelope girl to work that scheme—how sweetly she apologized for it!—I wonder what made her bother?"

And the Knight—"Pam's hair in the twilight!—That kiddie and her Wee Poor Things!"

And Cynthia—"I wonder why she thought of it? I always liked her, even when she heaved that screw-driver at me."

And Penelope—"What fun it all is! Wonder if I can purr like Peter. I must try to-night. How happy Twopence looks!"

And Twopence—"I'm in it! I'm in it!"

Then the Knight got up.

"Speech! Speech!" cried Timmy, beating his teaspoon violently on the table.

"*Sit down*, Uf!" implored Pamela.

"All right, old girl. 'Tisn't about us. I won't waste good ideas on that topic just now. No.—Ladies and gentlemen—"

"There's Peter, and Caramel, and Koosh," cried Twopence.

"And gentlemen—"

"Hear, hear! You have called Caramel and Koosh gentlemen!"

"I apologize and retract. Friends, I want to propose a toast. All sorts of secret schemes have been planned by certain people here, many, I expect, that haven't come to light. But some have— Pam knows one, and I know more than one, and we all know enough to be eager to drink to the health of our hostess and her sister—Penelope and Twopence!"

"Hurrah!"

Cups were raised as the guests sprang to their feet.

"For they're a jolly good fellow!" chanted Timmy, who was a little vague as to how the twins had helped to engineer the fortunes of his family, and was resolved to be particularly grateful on that account.

> "For they're a jolly good fellow,
>   For they're a jolly good fellow,
>   For they're a jolly good fe—ll—ow—
>   Which nobody can deny.
> Can you? Can you? Can you? *No!*
> Can you? Can you? Can you? *No!*
>   For they're a—"

It went on, for, as with such things, they seemed never to have too much of a good thing.

Twopence turned from Cynthia's smiling eyes and looked to see how her sister was taking it.

"It's glorious now, Penny," the look said. "We're even—in together. Aren't you glad?"

The grey eyes shone in answer to the demand made by the blue ones, and, under the table, Penelope and Twopence clasped hands.

"HIMSELF"
A Cat Story, by
Evelyn Smith

I

"OH, Auntie Betty, open the basket, quick! It's addressed to you, but it must be the kittens for *us*. Do open it, quick!"

Barbara tugged at the lid of the hamper, danced round it, clasped her aunt's arm, and, as Miss Maughan just smiled and pulled off her gloves, repeated, with something suspiciously like a whine, although she was ten years old: "*Do* open it—now."

"Can you hear them, June?" said Aunt Betty, kneeling down and putting her hand on the smooth little nut-brown head of her younger niece, who, lying flat on the floor, was pressing one ear to a space in the wicker-work. "Are they crying?"

"No; I think they're asleep, Aunt Betty. You'll take off the lid softly, won't you? Kittens would be frightened if they woke suddenly and saw all our faces—"

"They'd be frightened if they saw *yours*," laughed Barbara, with a little confident toss of her primrose curls. "It *is* kittens, isn't it, auntie? Kittens from Uncle George? It must be. He *promised*—"

"Perhaps it's a brace of grouse for me," said Aunt Betty, snipping the string of the label. "We'll have them nicely roasted on toast, with a little butter in their insides."

"Roasted on toast! Oh, Aunt Betty, look, look!"

Barbara plunged her hands into the basket and dragged out two kittens, nest of hay and all. They looked from side to side with bewildered eyes, a little dazed by the light and the voices.

One was a ribboned blue Persian, already in splendid coat; the other a smooth pinkish-cream and brown little creature, with a rather mysterious expression and a collar of bells round his neck.

"This is mine, the darling," said Barbara, pressing the Persian to her cheek. "He knows me already, doesn't he, then?"

June sat back on her heels and looked wistfully at Barbara and the beautiful little cat. Barbara was so quick and pretty and noisy and gay—she always attracted people's attention, and got the lion's share of petting and presents. Uncle George had

"'This is mine, the darling,' said Barbara, pressing the Persian to her cheek"

promised to send two Persian kittens, exactly alike, for both his nieces loved soft and fluffy and stately pusses. It was queer that he should have forgotten so soon.

"Couldn't we have half a kitten each?" she said.

Barbara opened her mouth and eyes.

"Half—a—kitten—each? Cut up kittens? You are a silly, June, and cruel, too."

"I mean, share them. They could just be *our* kittens till we go home. They'll be cats then, and Auntie Betty might decide which is to belong to which—"

"Barbara is to choose," said Aunt Betty. "Uncle George made that quite clear."

"Never mind, June!" cried Barbara. "It's because I'm older, that's all. And yours is quite a nice little kitten, isn't he?"

June looked longingly at the heap of grey fluff in Barbara's arms, and then, with doubt and disappointment, at the strange form of the other kitten, who having done his best to curl his short kinked tail about him, had made himself into a stiff sphinx-like image, and sat staring into the kitchen fire as solemnly as if he were a grown-up cat. Feeling her eyes on him, he turned his head, opened his mouth wide in a voiceless miaow, and again looked into the fire. Suddenly she was sorry she hadn't welcomed him, and, softly taking him into her arms, stroked his head and kissed him.

"He is a darling," she said, "far better than any cushiony cat. He's a little strong tiger, isn't he, then?—and he knows all the secrets, and doesn't care—and he has four gold bells round his neck, and his ears are like little black velvet chimneys—and he has a beautiful sealskin tail, a darling, a darling, the best little puss that ever there was."

"No," said Barbara, "*mine* is the best."

"What are you going to call them?" said Aunt Betty, who stood with her hands in her tweed coat-pockets, watching her nieces and smiling to herself because they were so like her eldest sister and her youngest.

"Mine's going to be 'Rex,'" said Barbara. "'Cause he's the king, the beautifullest cat of all the cats."

"Mine's 'Himself,'" said June.

"You can't call a kitten Himself," said Barbara, who, although generally she was very nice to June, couldn't help feeling exasperated with her every row and then.

"You can," said June obstinately, "'cause it's my kit's name. He's a smooth puss, and not a kingly expensive Persian; but he's Himself, and I like him because he is and because I do."

"Well, my kit is Himself, too, if you come to that," said Barbara.

"I think they're good names, both of them," interposed Aunt Betty. "And the kits must be so hungry. What about a saucerful of bread and milk for Rex and Himself?"

II

BARBARA and June generally spent most of their holidays with Aunt Betty, who, being a bachelor aunt whose great interests were dogs and cats and games, was a quite interesting person to stay with, and was not bored with the society of two small girls with tastes similar to her own. This year their summer holiday extended itself right into October, as Barbara was to go to Spain with her father and mother in November; and June, who had been ill last spring, was to be away from school until after Christmas. So they were still with Aunt Betty when the big autumn Dog and Cat Show was held at Mitchingham.

"D'you think I might show Rex?" Barbara wanted to know one morning, as she brushed and combed her beauty.

"Of course," said Aunt Betty.

"Oh, *may* I, auntie ? How lovely! I thought they wouldn't have young cats in—Rex'll be much more enormous and kingly and soft and beautiful in six months, won't he?"

"Well, they have a class for children's pets," said Aunt Betty. "It would be quite a good plan to accustom him to being shown while he is young. You must cover his cushion with blue silk, Barbara, so that the colour will set him off as he sits in his little cage."

June stood looking rather wistful as she softly rubbed her chin on the head of Himself. Even when she was standing up, she could make a comfy bracket for a kitten or puppy with her arms, and the mysterious countenance of her strange little cat was full of content. Barbara glanced at him.

"Oh, June, I'm sorry!" she exclaimed. "I wish Himself wasn't a sleek cat. I wish you could show him."

"But June must show Himself," said Aunt Betty. "Of course she must."

"They wouldn't laugh at him and say he's a piebald cat, would they?" said June in a whisper, in case he should hear.

"Laugh at him? I shouldn't care to laugh at him. He might summon some witch by moonlight to set a spell on me so that I should always laugh at the wrong time and in the wrong place, or turn me into a bit of fish or cat's meat, so that Himself might gobble me up."

"No, no, he wouldn't do that. He's only mysterious, he isn't wicked. He's a good, good little Christian cat, aren't you, darling Himself?"

"Well, he won't be a good, good little Christian cat if he gets jealous," said Aunt Betty. "So we'll show him, too, just for fun and fairness. And we'll cover a cushion for him with a bit of striped orange and purple and jade silk I have upstairs, and make his cage look like a jazz parlour. You'll see."

Barbara and June at once set about making cushions for the kittens, and Rex was presented with a splendid new blue ribbon.

June considered buying an orange one for Himself, but finally decided that he should wear his little collar with the four gilt bells. It seemed more suitable for him than a bow, she thought, and Aunt Betty thought so, too.

On the morning of the great day the kittens were groomed until Aunt Betty pointed out that, as it would be impossible to treat them with Tatcho or Harlene before the show, it might be advisable to leave a little fur on them. Greatly to their surprise and indignation, their eyes and whiskers were sponged and their small sharp teeth brushed. Barbara dusted some violet powder on Rex's back, and June sprayed Himself with just one squirt of eau-de-Cologne.

"Come, come," said Aunt Betty, "you'll have your pusses in vile tempers before you get them into their baskets. You're as bad as the little boy who painted his face with a pink tooth paste before he went to the party. Give them each a wee bit of liver to make them happy again, and then put them in."

It was a most interesting show. Barbara and June were overjoyed to find that they might carry their kittens before the judges, and play with them and coax them to be good while their points were noted down on little cards. Considering what felines are on such occasions, both Rex and Himself behaved with commendable calm. They would not put on their prettiest expressions or get into their most fascinating attitudes, but they did not disgrace themselves as did a big tiger puss called Tamburlaine, who dashed off the table on which he had been set and swarmed up to a dusty shelf above the cages, where he sat glowering, refusing to be cajoled down, accepting no apology. "He does that *every* year," said his owner, nearly crying with embarrassment and annoyance. "But I keep on bringing him, just in case he should get used to it, and win a prize."

When the judging was over, Aunt Betty took Barbara and June out to lunch in a pretty green and white restaurant with big windows. They had the things they liked best: lamb and mint-sauce, fruit-salad with heaps of cream, and glasses of fizzing lemonade; but they were too much excited to notice what they ate. Every now and then Barbara would give a little jump and say: "Oh, I *wonder* if Rex has a prize. I *wonder* if Rex has a prize. Surely he'd get a second, wouldn't he, auntie, even if that big tiger Tamburlaine comes down and gets a first?" And June would cry: "Oh, I *hope* Himself isn't lonely! I hope that cat in the opposite cage isn't sneering at him. I hope he won't mind if he sees other cats getting prizes—d'you think he will, Aunt Betty? D'you think he will? D'you think cats understand about being better-looking than one another?" Aunt Betty said that the odds were that cats were a lot more sensible and less snobbish than human beings, but, although she looked relieved, the expression of anxiety did not quite go from June's eyes.

At last lunch was finished and they were in the hall again. Barbara at once dashed to Rex's cage; June, more slowly, her heart beating, though she didn't know why it should, went to where a piece of orange silk sticking through the wires showed the lodging place of Himself.

No, it couldn't be! It couldn't! There must be some mistake. No—it really was true—it really was there—that red card on which was inscribed:

FIRST PRIZE
AWARDED TO MISS JUNE LOVEDAY'S
ROYAL SIAMESE KITTEN—HIMSELF

"Oh, Himself!" she said in a soft little broken whisper. "Himself! What d'you think of that?"

Nothing much, Himself seemed to say. He took it for granted. With pleasure and condescension he rubbed his head against the three fingers June pushed through the bars of his cage.

"You know about it, you wise one, don't you? You know you're a royal and champion puss?"

"Well, June, pleased?" Aunt Betty was looking down at her and laughing. By her side stood Barbara, rather crestfallen, but bravely trying not to show her mortification.

"Rex is Highly Commended," said Aunt Betty. "We have just been looking at him, and he's well worth it."

"But—Aunt Betty—I thought—"

"Of course; Uncle George wanted to give you two kittens of equal value—but, as it turned out, he could get one Persian and one Royal Siamese, and the Siamese happened to be the better of the two. He said the fairest way would be to let Barbara choose, as she is the elder, and she usually knows her own mind. And you *do* love Rex, don't you, Babs?"

"Yes, of course I do," said Barbara. "And I'm glad Himself is such a good cat; June. I'm glad he's got first prize."

She said it out well, though she was smarting with disappointment. June took her hand.

"P'r'aps Rex will get first prize when he's a *cat*," she said. "P'r'aps Himself won't be such a lovely grown-up as he is a kitten."

She turned and saw Himself looking at her, and went to his cage to speak to him.

"But you will," she whispered. "You'll be the loveliest grown-up cat that ever was, Himself, my darling Siamese puss, whether you win any more first prizes or not. You know that, don't you, Royal One?"

Putting his paw between the wires, Himself clawed his red card.

Books to Treasure

Old favourites

E M CHANNON:
The Cinderella Girl
A Countess at School
Expelled from St Madern's
A Fifth Form Martyr
The Handsome Hardcastles
Her Second Chance
The Honour of the House (eBook only)
That Awful Term

E E COWPER (eBook only):
The Mystery Term (Crystal 1)
The Holiday School (Crystal 2)
The Fifth Form Adventurers (Crystal 3)
The Invincible Fifth (Crystal 4)

Camilla's Castle

SARAH DOUDNEY (eBook only):
Monksbury College
When We were Girls Together

sales@bookdragonbooks.co.uk   www.bookdragonbooks.co.uk

EVELYN EVERETT-GREEN (eBook only):
Queen's Manor School

E L HAVERFIELD (eBook only):
The Ghost of Exlea Priory
The Discovery of Kate

RAYMOND JACBERNS (eBook only):
A A School Champion (Lyndhurst 1)
The Record Term (Lyndhurst 2)
Discontented Schoolgirl (Lyndhurst 3)

BESSIE MARCHANT (eBook only):
By Honour Bound
To Save Her School!
The Two New Girls

DOROTHEA MOORE (eBook only unless specified):
A Plucky Schoolgirl (Manor School 1)
The Making of Ursula (Manor School 2)
Terry the Girl-Guide (Manor School 3)

Brenda of Beech House
Fen's First Term
Head of the Lower School
Her Schoolgirl Majesty
A Runaway Princess
Septima Schoolgirl
Séraphine-Di Goes to School
Tam of Tiffany's
Wanted: an English Girl (print & eBook)
The Wrenford Tradition (print & eBook)

WINIFRED NORLING:
Monica of St Monica's (Monica 1)
An Imperfect Prefect (Monica 2)

The Quins at Quayle's

EVELYN SMITH:
Seven Sisters at Queen Anne's (Queen Anne's 1) (eBook only)
Septima at School (Queen Anne's 2)
Phyllida in Form III (Queen Anne's 3)

Val Forrest in the Fifth (Myra Dakin's 1) (eBook only)
Milly in the Fifth (Myra Dakin's 2)

Biddy and Quilla
Binkie of IIIb
The First Fifth Form
The Little Betty Wilkinson
Marie Macleod, Schoolgirl
Nicky of the Lower Fourth
The Small Sixth Form
The Twins at School

ETHEL TALBOT (eBook only unless specified):
The Girls of the Rookery School
Jan at Island School
The New Girl at the Priory (print & eBook)
Patricia, Prefect

THEODORA WILSON WILSON (eBook only):
Founders of Wat End School
The St. Berga Swimming Pool

eBooks available for download from all Amazon sites

Also available from Books to Treasure:

HELEN BARBER:
Mollie's Choice
The Princess and the Socks

PHILIP S DAVIES:
Destiny's Rebel (Rebel 1)
Destiny's Revenge (Rebel 2)

ADRIANNE FITZPATRICK:
Spirit Wings

WENDY H JONES:
The Dagger's Curse (Fergus & Flora Mysteries 1)

ELEANOR WATKINS:
The Village
A Wind of Change

A J WEAVER:
Be Quiet, Bird! (available for Kindle in French and German)
Big Cats, Little Cats

eBooks available for download from all Amazon sites

Lightning Source UK Ltd.
Milton Keynes UK
UKHW02f1441190718
325985UK00004B/40/P